Hero Revealed

Anna Alexander

Susan

May you get votely what you want but also what you need.

As a female sheriff in a small town, Brett Briggs faces enough obstacles turning complacent good ol' boys into a top-notch police force without the added insult of a vigilante apprehending her criminals. Her prime suspect? Kristos Kilsgaard, the sexy river guide who has been open in his desire to move her away from her badge and into his bed.

In his former position as royal guard, Kristos once failed a woman he cared for and as punishment was banned from his home on one of Saturn's moons. He vows not to make the same mistake with Brett and uses his superpowers to protect her, no matter the foe. Or the cost.

But Brett didn't become sheriff by letting a man take care of her, and although the hot-as-hell Kristos is persuasive, she's not going to start now—even after burning it up between the sheets with him. When her town is threatened, they cry out for a hero and she sets out to prove to everyone, Kristos included, that she's the woman for the job.

Dedication

For my Chicklets. I love you to Saturn and beyond.

Acknowledgments

I am fortunate to have a kick-ass support group in my family. Thank you for the unwavering faith you have in me in all my endeavors. Thanks also to my girls, Danielle Monsch, Crista McHugh and Gwen Mitchell whose talent and friendship push me to be a better writer.

Find Anna Online

Website

annaalexander.net

Facebook

facebook.com/pages/Anna-Alexander/282170065189471

Twitter

twitter.com/AnnaWriter

Newsletter

http://eepurl.com/Q0tsz

Chapter One

"**S**ON OF A bitch," Sheriff Brett Briggs cursed and struck her clenched fists on the wood desk. She sucked in a deep breath, biting back the rest of the expletives blistering her tongue. When her heartbeat slowed and the red in her vision cleared, she turned to the deputy seated to her right. "Play it again. Please."

Deputy Mick Collins arched a blond brow but said nothing as he typed the order on the keyboard.

Brett locked her knees and leaned in close until the electric hum from the monitor buzzed against her skin. From the corner of her eye she noted the time on the footage as 12:35 a.m. At 12:36 the suspect entered the scene, triggering the silent alarm that had notified the police of the break-in.

The picture was grainy and the light poor, but she was able make out the tall, thin, jittery shape of Trevor Conkle maneuvering through the construction zone that was the Anderson's kitchen remodel. He picked up a hammer that lay in the open tool box on the floor then attacked the drywall as if he were auditioning for Jack Nicholson's role in *The Shining*.

With the price of minerals at a premium, the copper pipes

running in the walls were like buried treasure. A one-foot pipe scored enough cash to keep a junkie high for a week. It was one of the many reasons Mr. Anderson installed the security system and video cameras during the renovation.

In Trevor's clumsy grip it took several strikes for the pipe to snap loose and fall to the floor. At 12:41 he danced a little jig as he snatched it up and cradled it to his chest. The metal never had time to warm in his palm before a shadow stole across the camera, whirling around Conkle like a specter. Blurs of black and gray pulled at his arms and lifted him off the ground.

Brett squinted, hoping this time she'd be able to make out something, anything that made sense. From its size and shape it had to be a man, but he moved like nothing she had ever heard of or seen before. In less than five seconds, Conkle was hog-tied and laid out on the tile floor. The film's resolution turned his skin a sickly green as the color leached from his cheeks. He looked like a bass out of water as he thrashed on the floor with his mouth opening and closing in silent screams.

One second the stranger was there, and the next, nothing but empty space. At 12:42 Brett entered the scene, gun drawn. Studying the tape, she felt her brow crinkle with the same confusion and frustration she saw on her video image. After three viewings she was still as baffled now as she had been when she found Conkle on the floor.

"Are you sure that man's not one of ours?" she asked Collins. Of all the deputies in her department, he was the one she trusted most not to jerk her chain.

"You were the first on the scene." His blue eyes rang crystal clear with sincerity. His lips pinched tight together, but in his eyes she saw the words she didn't want to hear.

Mother fucker, he struck again.

In through the nose, out through the mouth. Breathe.

"Where's Conkle now?"

"He's in the right one."

Brett snorted. When she was a cop with the city police, she had an entire floor of interrogation rooms at her disposal. Here in little Cedar, Washington there were two—the left one and the right one.

"Has he lawyered up yet?"

"A public prosecutor will be here first thing in the morning."

Perfect. "I need a moment with the kid, alone."

"Yes ma'am."

With each step down the corridor, her blood bubbled like the lava under Mt. Etna. This was the fourth time since she joined the department when she was the first to appear on the scene to find the perp trussed up like a Thanksgiving turkey without any clue as to how. No one in her department confessed to collaring her criminals and it hadn't happened to anyone else. But now she had video footage. Her ghost had a physical body, and a body could be traced. The only question was who was playing her, and why.

Brett stopped in her tiny office on her way to the interrogation room and retrieved a slim black case from her desk before stealing into the even tinier attached bathroom.

A brush of powder under her eyes covered the dark circles caused by working an endless string of eighteen-hour days, and a splash of blush across her cheeks gave her a healthy glow. Cinnamon oil in the lip gloss stung her lips and shot the scent up her nose like a jolt of caffeine to awaken the senses. The carefully applied makeup was a mask, as much an important part of her uniform as the latte-colored shirt and brown pants she had tailored to fit her curves. Every crisp detail emphasized she belonged.

She was the sheriff and one of the only women in the department. Appearance and attitude was everything when dealing with men who got a hard-on intimidating those they felt were weaker. One crack in her armor and her belly was exposed. All these months of hard work would not be wasted because she allowed some jack-off vigilante to jeopardize her credibility.

Outside the interrogation room she paused to look through the glass in the door. Conkle was slumped over in the metal folding chair, shoulders and legs twitching with the remnants of meth coursing through his veins. She opened the door and let the metal slam shut. His arms flailed wildly with his surprise.

"Hello, Trevor," she said in a low, congenial tone.

"Sheriff." He wiped at the drool on his chin with the sleeve of his flannel. "So when am I getting outta here?"

"The public defender will be here in the morning." She slid into the seat on the opposite side of the table and laid open the file folder she brought with her. "How about you and I have a chat?"

"Uh-uh." He shook his head so hard she couldn't tell if it was denial or meth shakes. "I'm not talking without a lawyer present. I've seen *The Shield*."

"If that's what you'd like." She closed the file and folded her hands on top. "Then I'll take you down to holding, but I have to warn you, it's a little crowded tonight. We busted up a bar brawl between a couple of 69ers and Demon Messengers. They weren't too pleased to have their trip to Sturgis postponed. I'm sure you can help them pass the time." She allowed a hint of a smile to play on her lips.

His skin paled, the veins popping out on his forehead. "Were they those biker dudes I heard shouting?"

Her smile widened. The animosity between the two biker gangs was legendary, but even more so were the stories of how they would band together for the simple pleasure of fucking with an outsider.

"Fuck." He dug both hands in his hair and rested his head on the table. "What? Just…what?"

The click of her pen echoed against the cinder block walls. "Why were you at the Anderson's this evening?"

He lifted his head to peek at her through his stringy bangs. "Uh, Mr. Anderson said he wanted me to help with his remodel?"

"He asked you in person?"

"Yeah."

"When?"

"This afternoon."

"Was this before or after his daughter's wedding?"

His forehead puckered. "What?"

"The Anderson's daughter was married today in California and they've been out of town." She narrowed her glare. "Cut the shit, Trevor. We have video footage of you tearing down the wall to get to the copper pipes."

"You do?" he asked, clearly confused.

"Yep."

He looked to the door then to the two-way mirror. "Then what's with all the questions?"

She leaned forward, eager to get to the heart of the matter. "Who tied you up?"

"Ah, geez." He looked up to the ceiling, as if searching for divine intervention and his cheeks turned a deep pink. "Some crazy psycho."

Her nostrils flared and she restrained the urge to slap him. "Be more specific, please. Think. You're in the kitchen. It's dark and the pipe is in your hand and then…"

"I don't know. It was like this—thing—came out of no-where and started grabbing at me. Everything was a blur and crazy and these big hands were pulling me in different directions, then I was just on the floor."

"Was it a man? How tall?"

"Yeah, I'm pretty sure it was a dude, and he was big."

"Did he say anything?" Her pen scratched across the paper as she took down his every word.

He snorted. "Yeah, he said, 'Let this be a lesson to you'," Trevor repeated in a deep register.

"Did you recognize his voice? Did he have an accent?"

"Not really. I don't know. It didn't sound like he did."

"What did he look like?"

"I don't know." He threw up his hands. "It was dark and I was being assaulted, plus he had a mask on. I could only see his eyes."

Brett grunted in frustration. "What color were they?"

"Weird."

She looked up. "Weird?"

"Yeah, they were this freaky, glowy green color."

Her heart slammed to a stop while her hand reached for the clear twine around her neck. Necklaces were prohibited while in uniform, which was why she wore the elegant circle low under her blouse where no one could see it. The cool jade laying between her breasts was a forbidden thrill, and only the wild, impetuous woman who lived in her darkest, secret inner self knew why she broke the rule. Not even under pain of death would she admit out loud to why she paid a week's worth of wages for the necklace.

The amulet spun in a slow circle as she held it up to the light. "Were they this color?"

"Yeah, just like that."

Green eyes that matched her necklace? Green like *his* eyes?

The papers rustled in her trembling hands as she gathered her things and wobbled to a stand. "Thank you, Trevor," she murmured and walked to the door. Excitement, dread and forbidden arousal stirred in her belly.

She had her suspect.

Chapter Two

B RETT TOOK THE corner at fifty miles an hour and accelerated out of the curve. The Crown Victoria held its ground as if it sensed her determination and didn't dare lose traction on the slippery pavement.

The parking lot in front of Cedar River Sport and Marine was empty of vehicles since the first guided raft tours didn't gather until nine. If she didn't strike now, it would be well after dark before she could question her suspect. The suspense was already grinding away at her concentration, spreading like poison ivy in an itch that desperately ached to be scratched.

A chime over the door announced her entrance. Harlan Kilsgaard, the proprietor, lifted his head from the morning paper and smiled in greeting. In his red-and-black flannel shirt, he looked like Santa Claus out for a spot of hunting. "Hello, Sheriff. You're a lovely sight on this dreary morning."

Normally a comment like that made by a man from Cedar was loaded with the expectation that she should bat her lashes and accept the compliment like a pat on the head for being a good girl, but Harlan had always treated her with the respect due to her position.

"Morning, Harlan." She smiled and wove her way through the display of fishing rods and canoe paddles and wet her lips with the tip of her tongue in anticipation.

"I heard you had quite a night with those biker gangs traveling through town. I hope they won't be passing this way again. Coffee?" He pointed to the urn behind him.

"No, thanks." She was so amped up she'd probably slosh the dark liquid all over the front of her coat. Wouldn't that make an excellent impression? "Unfortunately I don't think we've seen the last of them, but they'll think twice before stopping."

His wide smile bunched his white-whiskered cheeks. "I bet they will. So, what can I do for you?"

Now that the moment arrived, the words froze on her lips until she forced them out in a rasp. "I need to speak with your nephew."

"Lucian?"

"No." She swallowed hard. "The other one."

She hated to say his name out loud. Her tongue couldn't help but caress each syllable like a lover. When niceties commanded she address him by name, the dimple would crease in his cheek and his eyes sparkled with an unholy light, as if he had super powers and was able to pull from her mind the illicit fantasies she refused to act upon.

"Kristos?" A deep, lyrical voice spoke from behind her. "What has my brother done?"

Lucian stood in the doorway to the storeroom. The eldest

Kilsgaard brother was a drool-worthy hunk of man who had almost every woman under the age of eighty making comments about being the sole object of his regard. What Brett admired most about Lucian wasn't his incredible good looks but his kindness. He was respectful and spoke to her as a person, not a silly female. Honor and chivalry bled from his every pore. Women wanted him and men admired him.

Brett heaved a mental sigh. Oh, why couldn't her nightly fantasies be about Lucian? While she wasn't in a position to enter into any type of personal relationship, at least Lucian endeavored to be an upstanding member of the community, while his brother was the delicious bad boy, riding the rapids with an abandon bordering on suicide. Kristos lived as if there were no tomorrow, no responsibilities and no consequences. His ability to squeeze the enjoyment out of living down to the fleshy pulp drew his own large share of admirers. Most of them young and so bubbly they frothed over the tops of their shirts and out the bottom of their too-short shorts, which was why she became confused whenever his smoky gaze fixed on her. Why did he find her, an overworked sheriff, struggling to maintain the respect of the community, fascinating?

She'd never find out, because Kristos Kilsgaard was an indulgence she couldn't afford.

She straightened her spine and asked, "I have a few questions for him. Is he near?"

Doubt darkened Lucian's eyes. "He's in the back, preparing the kayaks."

"Thanks. If I don't see you again, have a good morning, Lucian. Harlan."

She circled the front of the store, slowing her steps as she approached the corner. Sometimes she imagined he had super hearing the way he always seemed to know when she was near.

With the rough-planked siding at her back, she crept closer, hoping for a moment of silent observation before alerting him to her presence.

"Good morning, Brett."

Damn it, how did he do that? She sucked in a breath for strength and stepped around the corner, and promptly swallowed her tongue when he came into view.

The morning sun highlighted the blue in his thick, black hair, making it look as soft as a panther's pelt. He was the definition of tall, dark and dangerous with his muscular build, confident stance and the double ring tattoo circling his bulging biceps. Adding to the air of danger was the wide scar bisecting the two bands. It looked as if a pipe had been heated and pressed to his skin, which had to have hurt. The mark matched the set of scars crisscrossing his back, which she only noticed because he often went shirtless, and not because the play of muscles made her lips burn with the need to soften the marks with wet kisses.

His thumbs pulled at the loops of his jeans, drawing her gaze to his flat stomach and well-worn fly. Her throat grew tight as she imagined cuffing him to her bed and licking every deliciously carved bronze inch. He sucked in a sharp breath and those pale-green eyes Conkle called weird seemed to see right into the heart of her, daring her to live out her most secret desires.

With all the grace of a newborn colt she stumbled forward and blurted, "What do you think you're doing?"

He gestured to the kayaks waiting on the river bank. His lips curled in that smug, obnoxious grin she itched to slap—or kiss—away. "My job?"

"I'm talking about last night and the week before. You're apprehending my suspects before I can and it has to stop."

"I have no idea what you're talking about." He cocked a dark eyebrow and replied with an accent as rich as hot fudge sliding warm and sweet down her spine.

"Don't mistake me for an idiot. I know who you are."

"I should hope so. I ask you out at least twice a week. I'm starting to think you don't like me." He chuckled and tilted his head with a frown. "You appear tired. Are you sleeping well? Come share a meal with me. How about we take the day off and go out to the lake for a picnic?"

"What? No—" She scowled and regrouped. "Whatever game you're playing stops now. I will not allow a civilian to interfere in police business."

"Ahhh." He brushed his finger alongside his nose. "You must be speaking of the vigilante I've been hearing whispers about. If you see him again, give him my thanks. You need someone to look out for your welfare."

"It's my job to take that risk. I will not allow such disrespect to continue."

"I mean no disrespect with my words, Brett. I'm quite aware of your strengths, however it pains me to think your light might be extinguished from this world before you've experienced all of the treasures she can provide, and I want to share them with you." His voice dropped an octave and her body trembled under his hypnotic spell.

Was his ability to make her melt and want to commit murder at the same time a gift or a curse?

He drifted closer, swaying in that way rock stars use to seduce their fans. Heat shimmered between them in waves, like sunlight hitting molten pavement. Her eyelids grew heavy as her limbs melted, softening in preparation of molding to his muscled contours. Under her thick down jacket, her nipples tightened, ready for his touch, and her hips shifted as wetness and heat pooled between her thighs. She was lost, drowning in the sea of lust radiating from his eyes and the promising pout of his lips.

"Why? Why are you doing this?" she whispered. "What do you want from me?"

A dimple appeared near the corner of his mouth. "I thought you knew. Apparently I've been too subtle." He leaned close, his chest brushing her coat. "I want you, Brett. All of you. I want your passion, your regard. I want you to loosen your tightly bound control and come apart in my arms with my name falling from your lips like a prayer." He ran the tip of his finger over her cheek. "I do love the way you say my name."

Cold air hit the back of her throat as she sucked in a huge breath, breaking the spell he wove with the sensuous grace that was pure Kristos. She shook her head and stepped back. "Wow. Such poetic words from a river rat. No wonder you have so many women lining up for what you dish out."

Crap. She mentally grimaced at the ugly snap in her tone. Why couldn't she wrestle her jealous shrew into submission? Kristos was a sexy man. His raw sexuality wasn't something he could turn off and on like a light. It wasn't entirely his fault that women responded to him with such shameless abandon, and she had made it perfectly clear she didn't want him. Lie that it was.

She wanted him so bad she sometimes trembled with the need and found herself, on occasion, with her keys in hand, ready to seek out his touch.

Kristos was like a well-aged bottle of bourbon. Hot and fiery as he slid over her tongue and down her throat, his heat permeating every fiber in her body with a sensuousness that stole all rational thought until she craved nothing but pure pleasure. Then the next morning would come the killer hangover and the painful pounding headache to remind her why she didn't drink in the first place.

He scowled as she retreated farther away. "That's not fair and you know it. Those women don't appeal to me, and do you know why?" He stalked toward her with purpose. Those big shoulders rolled with each step until he backed her against the side of the building, his heat and power invading her personal space. Crowding her further, he leaned closer so they were nose to nose. The warmth of his breath brushed her lips in a promise. "They're not you. You, Brett, are truly special."

A more naive woman would take his pretty, cultured speech as gospel and fall immediately in love with him. However, cynicism came with the uniform. She worked hard for her badge, and Kristos was always encouraging her to blow off her responsibilities. It took mutual respect and limitless patience to make a relationship work, qualities neither of them possessed.

Damn him for making her wish she were a different person than who she was.

She stuck a finger in his face. "This is my only warning. Stay out of police business. If I see you anywhere near a crime scene, I will Tase you. Do you understand?"

To keep him from seeing her shaking hands, she grasped her belt and stalked back to her squad car. Gravel shot from the tires as she sped down the road and away from her fondest desire. Her mother would call her crazy for walking away from the promise in his eyes. She, herself, questioned her own sanity during long nights spent all alone. Kristos didn't understand. Her mother never understood.

Cops did not make the best life partners. The hours were grueling, the pressure mentally breaking, and the few relationships that survived carried the possibility of being cut short by a gunman's bullet, just like what happened to her parents.

Since becoming sheriff her life had become a never-ending wave of uncertainty. She was still settling into a new community and battling the stereotype of sexism that should have gone out of style with parachute pants. The challenges she faced commanded one hundred percent of her attention, and Kristos said it himself. He wanted all of her, and she didn't have it to give.

That didn't mean walking away from him didn't hurt like a son of a bitch.

Her cell rang, reminding her there was more going on in the world than Kristos and his flirtations. She put in her earpiece and answered, "Sheriff Briggs."

"Sheriff, it's Marjorie Anderson. Do you have a moment?"

"Certainly, Mrs. Anderson. How was the wedding?"

"Oh, it was so lovely. Thank you for asking. The flowers were simply beautiful and the dress, exquisite. I must have taken at least a thousand pictures. But I'm calling to thank you for catching that criminal who broke into the house last night."

Pride filled her chest, making her sit straighter in her seat. This was why she loved her job. Knowing she was keeping her community safe made all the long, shitty nights worth the stress.

"Well you're welcome, Mrs. Anderson. Helping others is why I love what I do."

"And we're lucky to have you. And that masked man I heard was there too. If you see him again, will you send him my way? I want to make him a batch of my prize-winning brownies."

She barely held back the curse that sprang to her lips. "I— I'll see what I can do," she lied in a tight voice.

"Wonderful. Thanks again, Sheriff."

With a deep sigh, she shook her head. *Jiminy Christmas.*

Her belly craved something sweet and decadent. Since Kristos was off the menu, she drove toward the next best thing, a slice of chocolate cream pie at Betty Sue's Diner. Who cared if it was early? She needed it after the last twelve hours.

The jingle of brass bells and the aroma of bacon and coffee greeted her as she opened the door to Cedar's most popular establishment. As usual, her entrance garnered the attention of every patron. Since the minute she'd donned the badge of sheriff, she'd been questioned on everything from her moral values to her sexual orientation. Not once had she been asked about her views on public safety or how she planned on improving police procedure.

"Morning, Sheriff. Any word on that masked stranger? I hear he's physically impressive."

Ah yes, because when facing a potentially dangerous individual, she always stopped to admire their muscles.

"Morning, Judy." She nodded at the woman who was the head of the agricultural society, and the town's biggest gossip. "I have a few leads. How are the plans for the Arbor Day festival coming along?"

"I bet you can't wait to get your hands on all of those muscles. I heard he can lift a grown man off the floor with one hand."

"I can too with the right leverage. I'm not going to let anyone put themselves in danger. He's been lucky so far that he hasn't gotten himself or someone else hurt, and I'm going to make sure it stays that way."

Judy giggled. "You are so funny when you talk tough."

She let the statement slide off her back and said her goodbyes. She slid onto a barstool, resisting the urge to crumple in her seat.

Betty Sue set a ceramic mug before her and filled it with coffee, leaving room near the top for the cream and two sugars Brett liked. "I didn't expect to see you so early, Sheriff, after all of the hub-bub last night. I have to get your secret on how you stay so fresh-looking."

"I have stock in Oil of Olay."

"Oh, I hear you." She patted her blue-black French twist. An inch of silver roots ran along the part. "Me and L'Oreal are like this." She crossed her fingers. "So, what can I getcha? Your usual egg white omelet?"

"Actually, I would love a slice of chocolate cream pie. Just a little one."

Betty Sue raised a knowing brow and moved to the pie display. "Which male are we exorcising this morning?"

"Why does a male have to be involved? Can't I just want pie?"

"Honey, whenever a woman hits the chocolate this early

it's usually about a man, so it's either one of your dumb-ass deputies, that vigilante I heard is pestering you, or..." She flashed a huge grin and tapped her red-tipped fingernails together with barely restrained glee. "Perhaps it's a certain sexy river guide who's been after you since you moved into town?"

Brett stuffed a forkful of cream in her mouth to avoid answering. Betty Sue made it her mission to be Cedar's den mother and she treated Brett like her favorite cub. Betty's friendship and open spirit, not to mention the best fish and chips Brett ever tasted, made the diner one of Brett's favorite hangouts and she counted the older woman as a friend. However, there were some things she didn't share with anyone, and her feelings were at the top of that list.

Betty Sue set both hands flat on the counter and leaned forward. Her bold stare told Brett she wouldn't budge unless she heard a little dirt. "Let's just say that I think the Amazons may have been on to something."

"Don't give up on men yet, honey. They have their uses. And when I think of any, I'll let you know."

The women shared a laugh until the program on the television caught Betty Sue's attention. She let out a squeal and turned up the volume.

"It's the last episode of *Oprah*, people," she yelled out to the few remaining patrons. "So keep it down."

"I thought that show ended a long time ago."

"It did. It's in reruns now. I loved this one. It was so inspirational." She wiped down the counter, her gaze fixed on the screen. "Say what you will about the woman, but she does have a powerful message. Do you know how many people told her that she would be a nobody? Now look at her. And it's all because she listened to her heart and did what she loved. Kind of like us. We both worked hard at our dream and now I own this lovely diner and you're sheriff. Everything fell into place like it should."

Yes, professionally she set out to do what she loved and was able to achieve all she ever wanted.

Then why the hell did she feel so empty?

The bite of creamy chocolate settled in her stomach like a stone, and for the first time her solitary lifestyle felt like a worn-out corset, tight and confining with a stay sticking her in the ribs.

She pushed her plate away and faced the television, but her vision blurred. Tears she refused to shed burned the back of her throat. It was silly to cry over a man, especially a man who looked at her as if she were a rare treasure he coveted for his own.

No, she mentally shook her head and clenched her teeth. She made her choice. The people of Cedar depended on her to give one-hundred-ten percent of her attention. A job requirement she had been fully aware of, although hadn't quite comprehended the impact until now. Kristos could come at her all he wanted with those flexing muscles and smoldering eyes, but the people would always come first. Her honor demanded no less than her all.

Chapter Three

"KRISTOSLLANOS, WHAT HAVE you done?"

Kristos closed his eyes and sighed. Usually when Lucian called him by his full name a lecture followed. Fantastic, just what he needed, a second round of castigation. From Brett he'd take it gladly, his brother was another matter.

"It seems to be the day to be asked questions with obvious answers. I've prepared the life jackets and am now readying the kayaks." He tucked an orange plastic craft under his arm like a football and picked up two others, deliberately turning his back on his brother.

Lucian dogged his steps. "It's you, isn't it? You are this vigilante I've been hearing about. Just what do you think you're doing?" Lucian knocked the kayaks out of Kristos' hands and spun him around. "You know we cannot display our powers to anyone for any reason."

Kristos shook off the grip that would have broken a human man's arm. "I'm not displaying anything. The police presence in this territory is sorely lacking and Brett cannot manage the entire town on her own. I am only offering my assistance."

"Dashing around in a mask while endangering yourself

and others is not offering assistance. I know that you are capable of apprehending the average criminal on this planet, but have you given any thought about what will happen if we're discovered? I stood by you once and was banished from my home. I will not allow you to lose this one as well."

He clenched his jaw and spoke through gritted teeth. "And I will not allow what happened to Moira to befall Brett."

Lucian sucked in a sharp breath and jerked back as if kicked in the gut. "How dare you speak of our queen, may the Mother keep her, so informally. Sheriff Briggs is a competent woman who has been trained to handle the criminal element. If you must engage with her socially, then ask her out like any other human. Date her and be done with it."

Date her. It sounded so juvenile compared to the depth of his feelings for the lovely Brett. The good sheriff was a force of nature he found fascinating. The first time he saw her, she stood across from him on the opposite side of a busy street. Their eyes met and desire hit him like an open-palm slap in the face, while his two hearts beat in a rhythm he never before experienced.

Any other woman would have crossed the street to answer the invitation in his eyes, but not Brett. She stared right at him for several long moments. His empathic abilities picked up the desire her escalated breathing and bright blush barely hinted at. Then she frowned and walked away. From that moment on he was entranced, and with each encounter her mystery and allure ensnared him more. She was an intriguing dichotomy of strength and fragility, spontaneity and caution, passion and restraint that kept his attention riveted.

It frightened him to think that a wayward bullet or well-placed fist could destroy something so unique and wonderful. It was a fear he'd felt only once before. He ignored that warning and it destroyed his world. A mistake he would not make again.

"I don't want to date her. I love her."

Lucian's eyes bulged as he sputtered. "You do not. What do you know of love?"

"Brett is special, and I'm not giving up on her until she gives me a chance to win her heart."

Lucian crossed his arms and shrugged. "So you have feelings for this woman. That does not mean you risk our safety by exposing our powers."

His laughter rang with derision. "Risk our safety? We were born to put others' lives before our own, or is that something you've forgotten in your old age?"

Battle-toughened warriors used to bow to Lucian's authority. He had been fearless, decisive, and was the first to lead the charge against their enemies. Now he questioned every decision he made and spent more time with books and computers, learning about this world instead of living in it. Kristos' hearts ached with sorrow for the shadow his brother had become.

"Why are we here, Lucian?" He threw out his arms and gestured to the clear, blue sky and brilliant-green trees that covered the rocky terrain. "Look at this beauty. Feel the warm sun on your skin. If we came all this way to merely exist, then I would have gladly stayed and chosen death over banishment. I—we—chose life. Have you really experienced all this world has to offer? Are you going to hide forever? I'm not going to fear this world. I will eat until I am gorged, play until exhausted, and love until sated, because that is what it means to *live.*"

The mental wall Lucian threw up between them hit Kristos so hard, he wouldn't be surprised if he developed bruises on his frontal lobe.

Kristos opened his mouth to soften the blow of his harsh criticism when a wave of bubbles washed over his skin as his powers picked up the vibration of giggling girls. His nine a.m. river tour, a reunion of sorority sisters from Central Washington University. Fantastic.

He sighed and pinched the bridge of his nose, praying for the patience to survive the next three hours. When he looked up, he saw his brother staring at the rushing water. Deep lines creased his brow and bracketed his lips. Lucian's arms were crossed in front of him like a shield, with his hands resting on his biceps. The tips of his fingers stroked the spot where under his shirt lay a scar that matched Kristos' own. Loneliness weighed down his shoulders, pulling at Kristos' belly in sympathy.

"I'm sorry if my words hurt you, brother, but I will not hide. I'm not a fool, Lucian. I know my relationship with Brett is nonexistent. There's something holding her back from going after what she wants, but I'm not giving up on her, and I will not leave her without protection. She may not realize yet, but she needs me. If she arrests me for my efforts, then all the better. At least we'll be in the same building."

"And if our secret is discovered?" Lucian asked, his tone as stiff as his posture.

"Then it's discovered. We are *Llanos*. We've lived through hell. There's nothing we can't survive."

✦   ✦   ✦

BRETT PARKED HER Crown Vic and stepped out into a two-inch-deep puddle of mud. Since the brief bout of sunshine three days before, the skies had been nothing but gray and wet, leaving the earth a soggy mess.

A canopy of pine and cedar trees sheltered the small gathering of deputies. The wail of a siren echoed against the leaves as an ambulance and a fire truck pulled up alongside her.

She lifted her hand in greeting at Collins. "What have we got?"

"There was a small gang skirmish and the ground gave way, sucking two of the participants into the sinkhole."

"How far down are they?"

"Can't really tell. No one can get close enough without causing more of a cave in, but we've made contact and they're both conscious."

"I thought the last of the bikers left town days ago." She strode toward the flags that sectioned off the opening. "Who was fighting?"

"The Twihards and Vamp Diaries."

She looked back at him over her shoulder. "What?"

His features puckered as he nodded toward the circle of seven youths who appeared to be between thirteen to fifteen years of age. They huddled together in their leather jackets and Henley shirts while two of the girls sobbed, their tears leaving dark streaks in their white makeup. A boy, who looked to have an entire bottle of gel sweeping back his hair, awkwardly patted one of the girls' hands.

"Jiminy Christmas," Brett muttered and turned away. Her gaze met Collins' dancing eyes. He pursed his lips and gave a slight shake of his head.

The fire captain came to stand next to her and braced his hands on his hips. "Is that boy wearing makeup or did he have an unfortunate incident with a powdered doughnut?"

She sucked in a laugh. "Thanks for joining us, Captain. Okay," she barked, taking command. "Let's cordon off more of this area. I'm sure were going to have several upset parents arrive any moment and I don't want anyone else in danger. Collins, show me this hole."

The captain and two paramedics joined them on the trek over a small rise to a flat stretch of meadow. As she neared the gap, the earth sank under her feet.

"Sheriff, why don't you go ahead?" the captain said.

Brett placed one careful step in front of the other and knelt next to the two- by three-foot hole. She reached for the Maglight at her hip and shined it into the black depths. "Hello, it's Sheriff Briggs. Who's down there?"

"It's Caroline and Jacob," a small voice called from the dark.

"Caroline?" Something about the high-pitched female voice rang familiar. "Wait—Stacy Monroe, is that you?" A long silence followed. "Stacy?"

"Please don't tell my mom I fell in a hole."

She released a sigh of relief. If the girl could whine, then she had to be all right. "Honey, since your mother's the supervisor at the 9-1-1 center, I think she's going to find out. Who else is with you?"

"Just Jason."

"Are you all right? Are either of you hurt? Can you step into my light?"

A dirt-streaked face haloed in white-blonde ringlets appeared ten feet below. Stacy cradled her right elbow in her left hand. "My arm hurts and Jason can't stand. I think he broke his leg."

"Is he conscious?"

"What?"

"Is he awake?"

"Yeah."

She swung the light around and noticed that the girl appeared alone in the pit. "Where is he?"

"He's right there." She gestured to the shadows.

"Okay, honey, I want you to sit tight. We're going to get

you out. It's just going to take a few minutes." She turned back to the others. "Can one of you toss me a lantern?"

A small Coleman rolled in her direction. She flipped it on and lowered her arm down the hole. "Can you catch this?"

Once Stacy had her little light, Brett faced the group of men. "It looks like they're in some type of tunnel. Isn't this land part of Rainer National Park?"

"Yes ma'am," the captain answered.

Why would the state dig a tunnel in the park?

That was a thought for another time. Her first priority was to get those kids out without causing another cave-in. With only a few more hours of daylight left, the temperature was going to drop, and the sky looked ready to unzip at any moment and dump another inch of rain.

She rubbed her chin. "Collins, how long will it take to get a surveyor up here?"

"Thirty minutes, maybe an hour."

"They're about ten feet down. It would be nice to make the opening large enough to fit a stretcher, but I don't think we can wait that long."

"A back hoe will probably fall right in," said the captain. "We can send someone down in a harness attached to the wench on the fire truck to test the hole, but they'd have to be able to fit down that shaft, and light enough not to send dirt down on top of those kids. My guys are too big. Got anyone on your team?"

Four pairs of eyes turned toward her.

She didn't even hesitate. "Let's do it."

She latched the flashlight to her belt then stripped off her heavy coat. In five minutes she was fitted with a helmet and cinching a harness tight to her body.

"I know you're sending the woman down because you're afraid to endanger your penis," she joked.

"Damn straight." The captain laughed along with her men. "Now, we'll send you down nice and slow. Holler if the ground shifts, or when you're near the bottom."

"Right."

A crowd had gathered on the other side of the yellow police tape and more cars streamed up the road. Cedar was a pretty sleepy town overall, and news of the cave-in traveled as fast as a text message. With so many eyes on her, the pressure to execute this rescue flawlessly weighed on her as if she'd clipped an additional fifty pounds to her belt.

Suck it up, Briggs. You were hired to think on your feet and do the impossible. Now's the time to prove you're the man.

"How are you doing, Stacy?" she called out as she neared the entrance.

"Fine?"

"I'm coming down. Get as far away from the opening as you can."

She dropped a bag of supplies down first. The thud as it hit the bottom sounded way too far away. Adrenaline and a brisk breeze sent a shiver along her arms as she took that first careful step off the edge. Her hips scraped the sides of the rough walls and her breasts made for a tight squeeze until she was completely submerged in blackness. How one teenager, let alone two, managed to fall down the shaft confounded her.

"Stacy, how the hell did you two fit through this hole?" she hollered. "What were you doing?"

"We were running and Jason tackled me, and the next thing I knew we were falling. It was really dark and scary. Still is."

"Hang on, sweetie. I'm almost there."

Gravel and dirt hit Brett in the face as she dropped inch by inch. She closed her eyes and concentrated on keeping her breathing slow and even.

Her feet swung from side to side as she breached the tunnel. "Slow down. I'm near the bottom," she instructed through the radio at her shoulder. "Stop."

She unclipped the line and turned toward the lamp's soft glow to inspect her surroundings. The tunnel was about four feet high and eight feet wide.

The young girl had a bruise on her forehead but her eyes were clear and her pupils dilated properly when Brett flashed them with light. Her wrist looked swollen and had limited mobility. In the bag was a sling that Brett used to set the sore arm before approaching the boy.

"Okay, Jason, how are you holding up?"

"All right, I guess," he answered with a weak shrug.

He lay flat on his back, a purple sweatshirt pillowing his head. His dark hair and face were grimy and he shivered in the damp soil with what Brett hoped were the chills and not shock.

"Which leg hurts?" she asked.

"The right one."

With her knife she cut up the length of his denim-covered shin. "If you shift into a wolf, won't that heal your injuries?"

He managed a small grin. "I'm not really a werewolf, Sheriff."

"I know." She winked. "Just thought you might need a reminder."

A giant black-and-blue bruise circled his swollen knee like a bandana. Only an x-ray would confirm whether or not it was broken, but until then, Brett was going to treat him with the utmost care. From her bag she withdrew splints and straps and began to immobilize his leg. She kept him talking, pausing every now and again to update the crew of Jason's condition and her progress. When his leg was wrapped to her satisfaction, she carefully slipped the harness around his hips.

"Stacy, I'm gonna need your assistance to steady him while I lift."

"Okay." She kept her left arm tucked to her side as she helped Brett get Jason to his feet.

The slack in the rope tightened, which helped keep his weight off his leg, but he moaned and hissed as he was raised slowly in the air like a piñata.

Brett and Stacy ducked under the slate roof as gravel and earth rained down in small bursts. The trickle turned into a steady stream as Jason cleared the opening and the weight of the paramedics assisting him further upset the unstable ground.

The harness dropped back down and Brett helped Stacy pull it into place then stepped back to watch the next act of Cirque de Rescue. Stacy's squeaks and shouts as she pulled a reverse Alice up the rabbit hole made for a grating soundtrack.

An ominous crack shot an electric current down Brett's back, prodding her to action. She dove deeper into the tunnel as a slab of slate broke off from the ceiling and fell across the exit, spraying pebbles everywhere like buckshot.

"Sheriff! Sheriff!" Collins shout crackled through her radio. "Are you all right?"

"Yeah," she croaked. She forced out a cough then tried again. "Yeah. How about you all?"

"We're good."

"Great."

She closed her eyes. Fan-fucking-tastic.

Her lungs burned as she sucked in a mouthful of dust. Tiny streaks of daylight scattered in random patterns where it managed to find a fissure in the rock and soil. Unable to distinguish wall from ceiling, claustrophobia began to wrap her in its icy grip. Tiny, dark places reminded her of coffins, and thoughts of death were never good.

She jumped to her feet and mentally kicked her rising hysteria in the balls. Panic was going to help no one. Who knew when she'd be freed, and her time would be better spent gathering information to help her crew than to sit, wallowing in fear.

"Sit tight, Sheriff, we'll get you out."

She certainly hoped so. "Thanks, Collins," she said into her radio and wobbled to her feet.

Okay, first priority, ensuring breathable air. If she wasn't completely cut off from oxygen, she might take a crack at digging through that blockade herself.

Deep, dark and spooky, the tunnel stretched before her, lengthening with each step she took into the abyss. The temperature grew warmer the farther she went, but a cool draft skimmed over her cheek, which meant the tunnel had to have some sort of ventilation. The air was damp and tasted metallic on the back of her tongue. At five feet two inches tall she had to hunch over, but the floor was even and easy to traverse. As she walked, she trailed her fingers over the stone, noting the deep gouges that looked as if the rock had been carved out by a giant claw.

Her helmet bumped into a flat, square metal plate screwed flush against the rock. A few feet farther in, she found another. Their wide and irregular spacing set a wave of unease rolling in her belly. God, if those were all that kept the ceiling from tumbling down on her, she was in deep shit. After another couple of steps, the tunnel intersected with a second shaft that ran perpendicular to the one she came down.

"Hey, Sheriff." Collins' steady voice echoed down the tunnel. "How are you holding up?"

"All right for now. I'm definitely in a tunnel and it looks

man-made. I want someone to locate the permit for permission to dig in a national park."

"Dig as in mine? Ah, Sheriff, that may take some time—hey! What are you doing?"

"Collins?" Static. "Collins, what the hell is going on?"

"A man just jumped into the hole. He's—holy shit, did you see that?" The incredulity in his tone kicked her heart into fifth gear.

"What?" she shouted. Curiosity ate at her insides until her skin itched. "Collins, what's happening?"

"Someone's down there tossing—my God, did you see the size of that rock? He's tossing boulders out like they're pebbles."

She ran back to the blockade as fast as her stooped posture allowed. "Who is it?"

No response. Her heart crept up her throat with the suspense, cutting off further speech as she waited, staring at the wall.

A dirty hand reached through a thin crevasse and wrapped around a watermelon-sized stone and pulled. As the small hole in the blockade widened, she swung the beam of her flashlight and gasped as she caught sight of a familiar hooded figure.

Her vigilante.

A form-fitting black cowl covered his head and neck and continued down his arms. A tunic draped his torso and was tied at the waist with a belt like a karate obi. The metallic fabric reflected the fading daylight in sparkling bursts of light one second, then blended with the earth the next. Another rock was removed, revealing a pair of pale-green eyes that peered at her from the shadows.

Kristos.

"What do you…" Any reprimand she might have said died on her lips as she stared in shock at the impossible speed he used to remove debris.

"Sheriff, are you all right?" he asked, not even sounding winded.

She nodded then realized he probably couldn't see her. "I'm okay."

He pushed aside a boulder that should have taken a crane to lift. The grinding screech of rock on rock sent a shiver so cold down her spine she felt it in her teeth.

"You amaze me, Sheriff," he said, breaking through her stupefaction. "How you came down here without a moment's hesitation. That was very brave."

"It's my job. What's your excuse?"

The cowl obscured most of his face, except for his eyes and the opening that framed his sinful smile. "My job."

"Which is what?"

"Protecting you."

"I never asked you to."

"I know. That's why I do it. I will always protect you. Until my last dying breath."

She shook her head in confusion. His loyalty didn't make sense. They'd never been on a date, she refused him at every turn, they were practically strangers. His devotion was complete and utter madness. "Why?"

He paused, mid-crouch with muscles tense, and pinned her with an unflinching gaze, which left her feeling as if she were on a crazy roller coaster that was both thrilling and terrifying. "Because I think of you as mine, Brett. That fire, that passion you try to hide is a rare and beautiful thing. You are the sun that warms the cold loneliness of my days. You are mine, even though you push me away and won't let me love you, you are still mine. And if all I am able to do is protect you, then I will."

A tight band squeezed around her chest as she realized he meant every word. His interference had never been an issue about her ability or skill. He only wanted to care for her, any way he could.

Well, mother fucker. Her throat tightened as she fought to think. This adoration was a gift she had no idea what to make of. She was the rock, the dependable one who took care of everyone and everything. It was never, "How can I help you, Brett?" but, "Brett, please help me." To have someone do for her while knowing she wouldn't reciprocate was unexpected and left her at a complete loss.

She couldn't accept such an extravagant gift. His life wasn't worth her safety and she lived in constant danger. Could Kristos respect her position, or would he try to make her give up all she worked for to spend every night in his arms?

That doesn't sound so terrible, whispered her heart.

"It's time to go, Sheriff. Ready?"

She wet her lips. Was she? "Yeah."

His jaw went rigid as he clenched his teeth and pushed with his arms and legs. Ever so slowly the gap widened until she was able to squeeze between his hard body and the wall.

Halfway through, she was jerked to a halt as her belt buckle caught on the knot of fabric that circled his waist. Wedging her fingers in the nonexistent gap, she pulled and jerked at the fabric that refused to tear away.

"Hurry," Kristos hissed.

"I'm trying." She tugged harder. "I'm stuck."

"Holy Father," he groaned.

Brett glanced up and gasped at the lines of strain around his mouth and the amount of sweat trickling from under the cowl into his eyes that narrowed with pain. His body vibrated against her like a V-8 engine in need of a tune up and his arms trembled under the strain.

"I almost got it."

The metal snapped and she stumbled free, crashing into a pile of dirt. With a groan deep from his stomach, Kristos dropped the one-ton stone. The sides of the tunnel rumbled and quaked and dirt fell down on them like rain as the walls collapsed inward.

Before she could draw a breath, strong hands grasped her waist and tossed her high into the air and out of the hole. She hit the ground hard, rolling over and over until she came to a stop on her back. The treetops swirled above her as her vision swam. A heavy thud landed beside her. She turned to see Kristos flat on his stomach. Behind him paramedics raced in their direction.

"You fine?" he gasped.

She nodded, still struggling to breathe. "You?"

He frowned and his pupils dilated and constricted as if he, too, couldn't focus. "I don't know. Something's not right."

Now he recognized that something was unusual?

Despite whatever pain he was in, he pushed off the ground and rose to a shaky stand.

"I'll find you," he promised then ran for the trees at a speed that made his image blur.

Collins knelt next to her. "Sheriff, where are you hurt?"

"I'm fine." She batted his hands, her attention firmly fixed on the spot in the tree line where Kristos disappeared.

Collins followed her line of sight. "Who was that masked man?"

She turned toward him with a raised eyebrow. "Did you seriously just ask that question?"

"Well…" His cheeks turned red. "Yeah, but really, who was that?"

She opened her mouth to answer then looked back to the woods. "I don't know."

The statement wasn't exactly false. The "who" she knew. "What" he was, that was altogether different.

Chapter Four

WHAT WAS KRISTOS Kilsgaard? All during the examination in the emergency room, and later at the station as she completed her report, those four words played in her mind as if stuck on repeat.

What was Kristos Kilsgaard?

The doctor had given her a clean bill of health, so it hadn't been a knock to the head that made her see a lone man lift a refrigerator-size boulder and toss her into the air as if she were a Hail Mary shot before the buzzer in the Final Four Tournament. She could attribute the day's experience to stress, or lack of sleep, or it was dark and she missed her morning cup of coffee, but no, that wasn't true either.

So where did that leave her?

Brett rubbed the heel of her hand into her eye to try to alleviate the throbbing headache caused by constant thinking. Not even the hot shower and clean change of clothes she grabbed in her office gave her perspective.

Her house keys felt as if they weighed ten pounds and it took two tries to fit the correct one in the lock and push open the door to her little two-bedroom rambler. Without turning on the light, she shut the door and hung her coat on the peg on the wall.

She drew a deep breath as a thousand pinpricks of electricity scattered across her skin. "I don't remember giving you a key."

"I didn't need one."

A lamp switched on and she slowly turned around only to rock back on her heels. Kristos stood in her living room, freshly washed and so devastatingly handsome that the ancient Greeks would have thought him a god and made offerings to him daily. However it wasn't his beauty that held her enthralled, it was the worry and adoration in those amazing eyes that made it impossible for her to breathe.

"You know, I think I lost ten years off my life when I heard you were trapped." The low timbre of his voice quivered as his accent deepened. He kept his hands in his pockets as he took a step closer. "I could not stand by and do nothing when I knew I could help. You mean too much to me."

A thousand and one things gathered on the tip of her tongue, yet she couldn't utter the ones that logic dictated she should say. Kristos was not normal. He was possibly even…superhuman, which was a thought so incredulous she should be lying down with an ice pack to the head and a healthy shot of whiskey. All of her instincts were screaming at her to demand the truth, but at this moment, *this* moment, the barrier between thinking and knowing was as solid as a brick wall. Once she opened the lid on Pandora's box, the world and everything she knew about it was going to change forever. It was as certain as the color of her eyes. Whether she wanted it or not, her naiveté about the universe was going to die as soon as she got her answers.

Neither of them moved as he waited for her to respond. She licked her lips and fought back the panic that came with unavoidable change. She didn't want to know, not yet. It might be crazy, certifiable, but she wanted to defy the fates and steal a moment in time because his touch, his flavor, was what she craved. Her fingers flexed, ready to strip away the uniform that felt scratchy against her too-hot flesh. Beneath the lace of her bra her nipples tightened and throbbed in time to her rapidly beating heart. Need whipped through her like a live current, liquefying her center and making her all too aware of how empty her pussy was. Her throat constricted, trapping the words her passion-starved body demand she say. Did she have the guts to follow her heart?

Well, she didn't become sheriff by being a pansy.

"Kristos, will you love me?"

He cocked his head and blinked in surprise. "What?"

She placed a hand over his heart and felt it kick. "Make love to me. Please?"

He drew away even as he reached for her. Tilting her chin up with his forefinger, his brow creased with wariness, as if he could sense she wasn't one hundred percent confident of what she asked. "Are you sure?"

He wanted her, it was a fact he never denied, and yet he

waited for her to give the command.

With that act alone, the weight of a million doubts released, leaving her lightheaded but confident in her decision. "I've never been more certain."

She stood on tiptoe to run the edge of her tongue across his full lower lip before brushing her mouth against his with butterfly-soft touches. His eyelids lowered with drowsy desire. Chills ran across her arms as his fingers skimmed down her throat and cupped behind her neck.

"Always, *mi alskata*," he murmured, before fusing their lips together, striking a match to her tinder that quickly caught fire and raged into an inferno.

Dear lord, the man was hot. Not just in appearance, but his skin burned her through the cotton of his shirt and his kisses seared away anything close to a coherent thought. His heat sent her own temperature soaring and made her desperate for the feel of cool air on her naked skin.

She drew in his clean scent and reveled in the taste that was pure Kristos. He was like Irish coffee, smoky on the tongue, with a lingering burn that called you back for more. His kiss alone was worth the fall into madness.

He swallowed her gasp of surprise when he gripped the collar of her shirt and split it open with a jerk. Buttons popped like confetti to scatter over the wood floor, soon joined by bits of fabric so torn they wouldn't be fit for rags. Relief from being released from the coarse material was short-lived as a new hunger consumed her. She had to have him against her, surrounding her, pressing into her so deep she would never be free of him.

Surprise widened his eyes as he focused on her breasts. The backs of his fingers skirted up her quivering belly and traced the jade circle pendant that hung beneath the generous mounds. "Now this, I like."

Smug satisfaction entered that knowing smile, which always made her feel as exposed as an ingénue in her first *Playboy* spread. No matter how hard she tried, there was never any hiding her feelings from Kristos.

He claimed her mouth again, his tongue spearing between her lips in teasing jabs to tangle with hers in a playful game of hide and seek. Lifting her against his chest, he carried her the few steps to the dining table. Her bare back hit the cold surface and she arched with a hiss, thrusting her breasts into his waiting hands. His thumbs dragged down the cups of her bra, the lace scraped the pebbled tips that he soothed with the flat of his tongue. Pulling the nipple into his mouth, he suckled at the nub with deep draws that pulled straight to her core, making the ache in her pussy all the more unbearable.

"I want to touch you." She dug her fingers into his hair, which was just as soft as she imagined, as her other hand tugged at his shoulders. "Kristos, I need to touch you."

He smiled against her breast. "Hmm, decisions, decisions. Do I stop supping on these delicious breasts or have your hands running over my skin? That's a hard choice to make." He rubbed the thick ridge of his cock against the juncture of her thighs.

"Kristos," she growled and tore at the cotton of his shirt.

With a low chuckle, he stepped back and drew the shirt over his head. The soft lamplight threw every contour of muscle into stark relief, creating a road map of hills and valleys that lead to mindless pleasure. She pressed a light kiss to the scar on his biceps as she drew a line down the center of his abs with the tips of her fingers, then again with her palm. His shudder traveled up her arm, making her tremble in return. Leaning forward, she placed open-mouthed kisses against his blistering skin, drawing his salty taste onto her tongue.

"Brett. *Alskata,*" he panted. "If you go any lower—" He groaned as she blew hot air through his jeans over the head of his erection. Having the ability to make this big, strong man weak in the knees left her dizzy and eager to see how far she could push him.

She tugged down the zipper and sighed in delight when his heavy cock fell into her hand. Her fingers barely closed around the pulsing girth and her inner muscles clenched in anticipation of the sweet upward curve stroking along every nerve ending.

A pearly drop of pre-cum wept from the tip, which she swept away with her thumb. She wanted more of it, as much as he could produce, spurting down her throat, splashing on her breasts and deep inside her pussy. The desire triggered a quick flash of sanity. "Please tell me you have a condom."

From his back pocket he produced a foil packet and

slapped it on the table, leaving a hand-sized dent in the wood. His enthusiasm brought a grin to her lips before she engulfed the head of his cock and swallowed him down to the base. His taste quickly became one of her most favorite treats.

Against her tongue his cock flexed and pulsed as strangled moans stuttered through his clenched teeth. Her hands never stopped caressing him. The muscles of his stomach and thighs quivered under her palms. Each pass gave her the strength to give her body entirely to his keeping.

She could have sucked on him for hours, but Kristos wasn't content to let her take the lead for long. "No, no. I won't last."

He pushed her back onto the table and used his lightning-fast speed to strip her of her pants.

"By the Gods, Brett, you're—" He shook his head. "Words cannot describe how stunning you are."

It wasn't the words he used, but the light in his eyes and the flush across his cheeks that made her feel gorgeous, sexy and purely powerful in her femininity. Her legs fell wider apart and she skimmed her hands down her torso, her fingertips stopping just short of the blonde hair coving her mound. A siren's call to hedonistic oblivion.

The sound that welled from his throat was both animalistic growl and helpless abandonment. Open-mouthed kisses followed his calloused hand up the inside of her thigh. His thumbs parted the swollen lips of her sex, his tongue circling the nub of her clit before sucking it hard into his mouth.

Her entire body quaked under his ministrations and her teeth chattered with the adrenaline. She craved his possession, ached so badly she wanted to weep. Her pussy never felt so empty, so ravenous. Not even the thick finger he pushed deep inside slaked the hunger that built like a rushing river against a weak dam.

"More. Please. Please," she begged, grinding her cunt against his hand.

Her nails scored his back in an attempt to find purchase and avoid flying off the edge into insanity. His name fell from her lips like a chant one moment and a prayer the next.

"I love the way you say my name," he moaned and the sound vibrated against her clit. "Come for me, *alskata*. Let me taste you come."

Two fingers thrust deep and rubbed the spot inside that hurtled her off the precipice. The wave rolled up her body and exploded out the top of her head. Her vision blurred, only to clear when she felt the head of his latex-covered cock nudge her opening.

The last of her breath rushed out at the sight of the savage expression on his face. His eyes narrowed with purpose and the skin over his cheeks drew tight as the unrelenting grip on her hips readied her for his possession. Gone was the playful lover and in his place was an aroused man with only one thought on his mind. Fuck his woman.

His first thrust drew a scream, a sharp, high-pitched wail that robbed her of her ability to think. She was incapable of doing anything more than thrashing and whimpering under the onslaught of pleasure. The intensity in his set jaw and compressed lips held her captivated as he rocked the table with deep lunges.

"Put your hands over your head. Yes," he grunted when she complied. "Grab the edge of the table. Show your body to me."

His pupils dilated so wide only a thin, glowing green ring of iris remained. How wanton must she look with her legs splayed wide and his thick cock splitting her in two? Her bouncing breasts hung out of the torn cups of her bra, yet she didn't feel embarrassed as his cock swelled and sweat poured down to where their bodies joined. She was a willing vessel of gluttonous sexual need and he was rocketing her to a high she knew would become addictive.

His grunts and moans turned into mumbled words she didn't understand. The cadence was beautiful and she felt a warmth bloom in the center of her chest, growing and spreading like warm honey down her limbs to her tightening sheath. He placed his palm over her heart as his fingers cupped her breast, kneading her flesh while his chant grew stronger.

It was too much. Every blood vessel was going to rupture under the pressure, and her heart was going to pound right out of her chest and into his hand.

His head dropped back and his face slackened as his shaft jerked with his release, yet his hips continued with the relentless, driving rhythm and he demanded, "Take all of me and give me all of you."

He wasn't talking about her orgasm or her body. He wanted her soul.

Shock slammed into her at the same time she burst into a million fragments of light and sparks. An invisible rope coiled around them, binding them together as one unit, one heartbeat, one soul. As her pussy rippled in orgasm around his shaft, a tiny shred of self-preservation kicked in and tethered her to reality. She might have flipped a definitive middle finger to caution, but the dream was going to come to an end. He owned her pleasure, but her heart would remain firmly in her keeping.

With a final cry, he fell forward, blanketing her with his heat. He nuzzled the skin under her ear and murmured, "I knew it would be like this with you. Exactly like this." His small chuckle made her think there was a joke in there somewhere, but her brain was too scrambled to begin to guess what it was.

"I think you've killed me," she whispered, running her hands down his spine, hesitant to break the connection though she knew she should.

His deep laugh vibrated down to his cock that was still hard inside her. "Then they can bury me beside you. Come, let me take proper care of you."

He carried her to the bedroom and pulled back the covers on her bed with one hand. Goose bumps erupted over her skin when her back hit the cool sheets until he climbed in next to her and took away the chill. He pulled the comforter up to her chin and wrapped her in his arms. In seconds, he was fast asleep.

The dark crescent of his lashes looked incredibly long on his cheeks and drew attention to the dark circles under his eyes. She hadn't forgotten he had been ill after he pulled them from the tunnel. The frantic bout of lovemaking might have indicated otherwise, but Kristos was not at his full strength. Her smile trembled at the corners. Heaven help her if he had been.

Careful to not wake him, she leaned forward for a soft kiss. A tear spilled down her cheek and pooled between their lips, turning the kiss salty and bittersweet.

Slipping free from his hold was easier then she anticipated, which only spoke of his exhaustion. Fatigue beat at her as well, but she knew sleep would be as elusive as catching smoke.

She collected a change of clothing and escaped into the bathroom, purposely turning away from the mirror. She couldn't handle seeing the woman who had been taken to a depth of ecstasy she would never see again.

The soft yoga pants and t-shirt weren't classy, but sufficient for the cause. Instinct told her that the inevitable confrontation was going to get heated, and she did her best thinking when she was fully dressed.

After gathering a few essentials from the living room, she returned and sat in the armchair in the corner of the room. She may doze for bit, but when he awoke she'd be ready.

Chapter Five

K RISTOS BIT BACK a moan as every muscle in his body throbbed in both pain and pleasure. Something in that mine affected his powers and damn if he knew what it was. It was as if a sickening lethargy settled in his limbs, sapping him of his strength. It made him feel...human, or at least how he imagined a human felt, which was something that didn't sound all that horrible. However, he needed all of his powers in top form if he was to have a mate as stubborn as Brett.

He smiled and settled deeper into the pillows as he remembered the look on her face when he spoke the words that bound them together forever. She might not have understood the actual words, but she comprehended their joining was more than just fantastic sex. Her heart had been in his hand and her body milking him dry in the most explosive orgasm he had ever imagined. All that was needed to complete the ritual was her mind to meld with his and they would be bonded.

On his planet of gases and ice, it was easier to communicate empathically than with words. When a man and woman mated, their emotions weaved together like a tapestry, enabling them to sense their spouse no matter how far apart they may be. It was a private ritual where each person gave the other their entire being, mind, body and soul, in an exchange of trust so profound that it left a physical mark more permanent than any ring. A union like that was not taken lightly, and many of his kind never found that someone special enough to speak the sacred words.

As he anticipated, Brett shut down at the last moment, preventing the connection to complete. Disappointment of her rejection was fleeting. It was only a matter of time before she accepted him as her other half. Of that he had no doubt.

Smiling again, he reached for his woman, only to find emptiness at his side. The sheets were icy to the touch and his hearts dropped into his stomach. Had the night before been a dream, an illusion caused by the mysterious illness? Please Gods, let it not be so.

He jerked upright, half afraid to find himself alone in his giant bed with only a pillow for company, or worse, alone in Brett's bed while she was off placing herself in danger.

His eyesight adjusted to the soft light coming from a lamp on the nightstand that was, thankfully, not his. Brett's room, blessed be. He started to relax then straightened in alarm when he spotted her in the shadows.

The woman sitting in the chair with deceptive casualness was one he was all too familiar with and shouldn't have been surprised to see again. Yes, it might have been arrogant to think one fiery encounter would shatter all her reservations where they, as a couple, were concerned, but he had hoped that by making love, some of the ice she harbored around her heart would melt. Despite the appearance of the beginnings of his mark, she was still miles away from true acceptance.

Although not in uniform, she was definitely in full sheriff-mode, with her hair pulled in a tight braid and her body clothed from neck to ankles. She was glacier still, and the calm determination he sensed coiled inside her had both his hearts beating in triple time. He wasn't sure what concerned him more, the purpose he saw in her eyes or the loaded Glock that lay in her lap.

"Hey, there you are." He flashed what he hoped was his sexiest smile and held out his hand. "Come back to bed, *alskata*, I'm cold." Just because he knew there was a storm brewing didn't mean he had to acknowledge it.

"What are you?"

It was difficult not to flinch at the subtle emphasis placed on the word "what".

"I'm sleepy and aching for you." He patted the mattress. "Come back to bed."

Her hand covered the gun's grip. "What are you?" she asked again in a smooth, even tone that set him on edge more than if she had shouted.

"What's with the gun, Brett?"

"I'm being cautious. What are you?"

"Do you honestly think I'm a danger to you?" He battled with the flare of hurt sparked by her fear. "Why did you let me touch you if you thought I would hurt you?"

Her eyes darkened and her throat worked as she swallowed. When she answered, the vulnerability in her voice sliced through his hurt. "I—I wanted to know what it would be like to be with you when you were still just a man."

"I am just a man."

"I'm not stupid." She jumped to her feet with a shout. "What are you?"

Kristos sighed. The time had come. Revealing his true self was a gamble. Not only was he putting his future with Brett in jeopardy, but if his brother had any idea what he was about to do, Lucian would be pounding down the door and demanding his head. But Lucian had never loved another as Kristos did Brett, and some things were worth the risk.

He nodded and tightened his grip on the sheet at his waist. Now he understood why she was completely dressed. He was vulnerable enough, exposing his soul, without the added disadvantage of his cock straining for attention only she could give. "I'll tell you everything, but may I get dressed first?"

She gestured to the neatly folded pile of clothes at the foot of the bed and turned her gaze to the door. He hid his smile. Clearly this was all the privacy she would afford him.

She couldn't hide the brief flare of lust that hit him like a flash of heat when he got out of bed and pulled on his jeans. Using that to his advantage, he deliberately left his chest bare. She still hungered for him and he wanted her to remember that.

"You can put the gun away. I'm not going anywhere and

you know I would never harm you."

She glanced at the gun then back at him. He heard her heart race as she carefully set it on the table, and released a deep sigh as she waited for him to begin.

"Brett, I—" He raked a hand through his hair. Damn, this was harder than he anticipated. "I—Can I get you something to drink first?"

Her brow raised as her lips tightened to a thin line.

"Right." No more dodging. He took a breath and looked her in the eye. "I'm not from here." Her nostrils flared and he felt her surge of anger before he blurted. "I'm from Saturn."

Nothing. Not a twitch, not a scream, he couldn't even read her emotions. It was as if she slammed a door between them, leaving him alone in the cold.

"Explain," she requested softly.

"Lucian and I are from Skandavia, the second largest moon. The one your people call Titan. We were banished from our home and came to live here a few years ago."

Her tongue flicked out to wet her lips, but he was too preoccupied to appreciate her natural sex appeal. She motioned for him to sit on the edge of the bed before taking her own seat across from him.

"Explain banishment," she said in that calm, cool voice that was beginning to scare the shit out of him.

"Lucian and I are *Llanos*. Our family has been a part of the royal guard for generations. Even though guarding the royal family is a tradition for my ancestors, it is a title that must be earned, and our placement is based on skill, knowledge and ability. I guarded our queen and Lucian our king."

Brett listened to every word he said with such intensity that the urge to laugh welled in his chest. Only his Brett would learn there's an alien in her home and wait for all the facts before rendering judgment.

"Over the last few cycles our planet has faced many challenges. The weather has not been kind, and like here, technology and resources divide the haves from the have-nots. When people fall on hard times, there is always a faction who think they can do better and call for revolution."

As he talked, the wounds of yesterday reopened and caused his throat to constrict. He never opened up to anyone about what had happened, not even Lucian, who lived through the nightmare with him. So many nights he lay awake and imagined all the scenarios that could have, should have, gone differently. Only thoughts of the future kept him sane. A future with his woman safe at his side.

With Brett sitting so close, he wanted to hold her as he continued his story, but settled for the soft brush of her knee against his.

"Queen Moira was a magnificent woman who was incredibly beautiful, both inside and out."

Fondness touched his smile as he recalled the grace in her bearing, the generosity of her spirit and her skill at manipulating the men in her life. There wasn't a one of them who denied her anything, except for Kristos, which was why he was chosen as her personal guard. He gave her just enough freedom to be with the people who were her life's blood but was firm when required. His respect for her earned her regard as one of her most trusted advisors. She was a mother and friend to him when his position allowed none.

"She loved her people and hurt when they suffered. In the hostile environment, speech is sometimes impossible. Our people communicate through empathy, so the strife caused her physical pain that worsened with each day. The violence escalated and many innocent people were either killed or lost everything. The princess, who was the only heir, disappeared and our queen fell apart. She wanted to meet with the dissidents to talk to them, make them see that the monarchy wanted what was best for all Skandavians. I forbade her from going. Lucian as head of the guard forbade her. The king outright refused to listen to such a plan that involved her being anywhere near the Revolutionaries."

He paused and fought back the swell of emotion that strangled his throat. He was *Llanos*. Immovable. Nothing had swayed him from his oath of protecting the queen.

Much like Brett would not be swayed from hers.

He snipped the tether of understanding and focused on her sweet face. "Thirty seconds. That's all it took. I left her alone for thirty seconds so she could partake of her meditations. When the queen sought the solace of our Gods, I always respected her privacy and allowed her to block her emotions." His hand rested on his stomach as the rolling, sick sensation he remembered from that night returned. "Thirty seconds after she took to her chambers, I knew that all was not as it seemed. With help from her lady's maid, she had fled from the fortress to meet with the dissidents. I and my fellow guards followed right on her heels, but we were too late. She was killed and put on display as a show of power for the revolutionaries."

She hadn't just been killed, she'd been savagely brutalized. The image of his beautiful queen, butchered and hanging in the square as a warning to all, still haunted his dreams.

"The uprising ended soon after that," he continued, his voice thick with the tears he never shed. "Many felt that the extremists had gone too far in harming the queen, when their real issues had been with the king, and withdrew their backing. The lady's maid was executed for her involvement. As the queen's protector, I was just as much to blame for her death as those who slaughtered her. I was given a choice. Execution or banishment."

For a week he had been publicly stoned and beaten in a ceremony that the entire kingdom had been invited to participate in. The king stripped him of his sword and after heating it in the fire, sliced through the double ring tattoo that marked his status as guard to the queen. It was the cruelest cut of all and one he completely deserved.

Lucian argued for his life to be spared. His brother understood that Kristos would have gladly given his life for Queen Moira to be spared, but King Renauld was bonded to his wife and felt her loss with a depth of grief Kristos only now began to sympathize, while Lucian, ah Lucian…

"When Lucian argued in my defense, he too was relieved of his title and joined me in my fate. As you can see, we chose banishment."

Kristos kept his attention on a dark spot in the hardwood floor. His brother gave up everything for him and in the process lost himself to guilt and self-recrimination. Perhaps he should have chosen death and spared Lucian so much pain.

But then he wouldn't have met his Brett.

A knot released in his gut. His brother was in control of his own fate in this world, no matter how much Kristos wanted more for him. Whatever else happened in their future, Kristos couldn't regret coming to this world and loving this woman.

"Why did you choose Earth?" she asked.

He finally met her gaze and fell a little more in love with her. She leaned forward in her seat, hanging on his every word. There were no accusations in her eyes, no blame for his failures. Her sympathy and compassion wrapped around him like a physical hug filled with sunshine. It gave him hope for them.

"Lucian chose Earth because it was the closet planet similar in ecosystems to our own. On Skandavia our weather is more extreme and rain comes in the form of gases rather than water, but the atmosphere and ecosystems are very close, except where our physical abilities are concerned."

The mention of his superpowers snapped her spine

straight. "What exact powers do you have? You mentioned the empathy part, but do all of your people have powers? Are there more of you here on Earth?"

He couldn't hold back his chuckle. She was too adorable with the rapid-fire questions, although she would probably kick his ass if he said that out loud.

"While my people have the capability for interstellar travel and often travel from one moon to another, I don't know if any have come to Earth. As far as my powers, on Skandavia, Lucian and I were normal men. We were warriors who had great physical strength but nothing like we do here. Lucian believes that it is the Earth's gravity that has heightened our normal physicality. Our power for empathy is greater, as is our speed and strength. I can't fly or shoot webs out of my wrists, but I can jump a short building in a single bound." He winked at her and the ball of uncertainty in his chest eased when she smiled in return.

This connection they shared had the potential of working out. She was still there, unafraid and apparently fascinated by his tale. Euphoria didn't begin to describe the relief he felt at her interest. He wanted to pull her into his arms, stretch beside her on the bed and answer any question she had while he ran his hands over her body. Acceptance was the first hurdle. Once that passed she would become his mate and their life together could begin.

"I want to tell you everything about my world." He held out his hand, encouraging her to join him.

Hesitation clouded her features and the consideration she gave his outstretched hand gave pause to his inner celebration.

Patience. It wasn't his best quality, but when what he wanted was worth his life, no obstacle was too great.

He held his breath until he almost passed out before she slowly lifted her hand. The heat of her skin hovered over his upturned palm when the rattle of metal on wood erupted from the dresser.

Brett jerked back with a gasp and reached for her phone, breaking their tentative connection.

"Briggs."

"Sheriff, its Reutgers." Kristos could hear the deputy shout over the line even without his super hearing. "There's been another cave-in at the National Park. It's about a half mile south of the last one."

She jumped to her feet and reached for her gun, pushing it into the waistband of her pants. "Anyone injured?"

"Not that we can tell."

"Who called it in?"

"Rangers thought it was an earthquake, but then a dust cloud rolled in that obscured everything. When they went to investigate, they found the trench."

"I'm on my way."

Kristos jumped in her path as she raced for the door. It took all of his considerable strength not to shove her back in her chair and tie her down. "Where are you going?"

"There's been another cave-in." She pushed him aside on

her way to the door.

"You're not going. It's not safe."

She froze with her shoes in hand and leveled a glare at him that was icier than a Skandavian glacier in mid-winter. "You did not just say that."

"You are in no condition to travel. You've been in a cave-in, you haven't slept, and it's not safe."

"This is my job, Kilsgaard. The people of Cedar count on me to protect them. It's my duty and you, of all people, should understand that."

"Of course I understand, don't you get it?" he shouted after her as she stalked to the living room, hopping from one foot to the other as she slipped on her boots. "My queen was doing her duty and was slaughtered for it. I will not let you suffer the same fate."

She choked and sputtered as she turned to face him with fire in her eyes. "Let me? Who do you think you are? Just because you fucked me does not give you any control over my actions."

"Don't say that. We made love. It meant something to me. You mean something to me."

"That still does not give you the right."

"I forbid you to leave this house."

In one fluid motion she pulled the Taser from her belt and leveled it at his chest. "Are you faster than a Taser probe?"

Anger and pure feminine fury lashed out at him like a cat-o-nine-tails. With her valor he almost believed she was strong enough to handle any obstacle thrown at her, but he knew better. Still he found her fervor incredibly arousing. As fear for her soured his stomach, his cock reared to attention, ready to claim that passion as his own.

"Please. *Alskata*, my hearts, I beg you, don't go."

"Fuck you, Kilsgaard. I would never tell you how to attack a class five rapid, because I trust in your ability to do your job. Why can't you trust in mine? If I see you at the site, if I even think you are at the site, I will have you arrested and throw away the key. Do you understand that, E.T.?"

She snatched her sheriff's coat off the rack and jerked open the door. "Do not be here when I return. You broke in, I assume you can lock up behind you."

A painting of a mountain crashed to the floor as the door slammed on his gloriously infuriating tempest.

He gritted his teeth and fully prepared to chase after his woman then skidded to a stop at the door. Yes, no woman on Skandavia was like Brett. He had no doubt that if he followed her, she would shoot him without hesitation.

He pulled at his hair, and then bellowed in frustration. The front window rattled under the pressure.

Borrowing Brett's favorite expletive, he shouted, "Well, fuck!"

Chapter Six

"**N**O WAY WILL that son of a bitch alien tell me what to do," Brett fumed as she pushed her Jeep Cherokee past sixty on the twisting dirt road.

Tires skidded on the soft embankment as the truth of what she said sank in and her mind disconnected from her body for a brief moment.

Alien. Kristos was an alien.

She jerked the car back on the road and placed a hand over her racing heart. Kristos was an alien. As inconceivable as it might be, there was no reason to doubt his tale.

That's probably why he's an out-of-this-world lover.

She groaned at her own joke and pounded her head on the steering wheel a few times before sitting upright and drawing a deep breath.

His fear for her safety stemmed from the past, that she understood. He loved his queen and it was obvious her death continued to haunt him. It was exactly why she wanted to avoid a serious relationship while she was still on the force. She couldn't promise to spend eternity loving a man if every day she willingly placed her life before others. It wasn't fair and just too cruel. Knowing there was a family waiting to love her when she came home each night would always make her second-guess her choices, and as a cop the slightest hesitation would most certainly get her killed.

And the jerkwad knew that. He was exactly aware of the types of sacrifices required when such a vow was made, yet he forbade, actually *forbade* her to continue her life's work because he said so. Why? Because she was a woman? Because he thought of her as *his* woman? What gave him the right? They weren't dating. Their entire relationship to this point quantified as nothing more than a one-night stand.

That realization made her grip on the steering wheel slacken as her vision blurred.

Kristos made her want. She knew when she kissed him that the night was not going to end with cuddling and breakfast in bed, yet when her phone had rang earlier, she almost didn't take the call. His life story was fascinating. He was loyal and brave, and the passion he had shown her was beyond anything she ever imagined. That type of attention was addictive and a soothing break from the stress of her job. Each second spent in his company made her crave more of his loving attention.

She liked him. Really, *really* liked him, and fighting was both exhausting and a waste of their time. But his insistence that she change who she was cut her to the quick. All of her professional life had been spent fighting for the respect that others, men mostly, had been freely granted. Once, just once, could someone believe in her without having her run through an obstacle course to prove her worth? Nothing riled her more than being told she wasn't good enough based on a personal preference and not her actual ability. If Kristos continued to stand in the way of her doing her job, any possibility of them becoming a couple was as likely as a stripper keeping her clothes on.

Blue and red flashing lights snapped her out of her introspection. She mentally gathered all the fragments of her out-of-control reality and tied them up with a sturdy knot and shoved them into a deep pocket of her brain to process later. She had to focus on the task at hand, and an overbearing, well-meaning alien with super strength, super speed and a super cock was not at the top of her priorities.

A tittering laugh escaped. Yep, in her fucked-up world she had bigger issues to contend with.

With her resolve firmly in place, she arrived at the scene just as the sky lightened to a deep-purple haze. Dust hung in the air in a thick curtain, and a wide swath where trees once stood cut through the forest like a reverse Mohawk. Trepidation burst forth like a periscope bursting from the ocean to scan for hidden danger. This wasn't just a simple cave-in.

Brett smoothed back the fringe escaping her braid with one hand while she reached for her coat with the other. She really wished she had time to put on her uniform, but she knew if she hadn't gotten out of the house immediately, Kristos would have tied her to the bed, and no, that would not have been a good thing, she admonished her traitorous libido.

Deputy Reutgers approached her as she stepped from the vehicle. He was young but eager, and hadn't fallen into the complacency of policing a small town like some of the other officers had. She had high hopes of him being a big part of the next generation of the department she was working so hard to reinvent.

"Morning, Sheriff." He tipped his hat in greeting then his jaw dropped in alarm. "What happened to you?"

"What are you talking about?" She frowned then tried not to wince as she imagined what she must look like. Shit, had Kristos left a hickey she hadn't noticed?

"Your eyes," he stammered and pointed at her face.

She bent to look in the side mirror and choked on a gasp. She blinked once, twice, then three times in hard, tight pulses, but the image didn't change. How the hell had she not noticed that?

Her irises, once a plain, nondescript hazel, were now milky white.

A string of curses that would've made a Hell's Angel blush rent through the morning air, scattering whatever remaining wildlife in the area scurrying for their lives. Her fingers dug into the cold metal around the mirror as she wished it was the neck of a certain alien from Saturn.

He did this to her, whatever *this* was. He must have.

"Sheriff?" Reutgers asked. She didn't miss the way his hand covered his privates, as if he expected her to pummel the first victim she encountered. With the anger surging through her, it was a very real possibility.

"It's, ah, it's a…uh bandage the doctor gave me for some scratches on my eyes. They're like contacts. I just didn't expect it to look so dramatic."

"I didn't know that even existed."

"Modern medicine for you." May the boy be kind enough not to question her further. "Show me what's going on."

A handful of park rangers and a few of Cedar's finest stood where it looked like Willie the Giant dragged his trowel in the ground in preparation for planting.

She let loose with a low whistle as she surveyed the damage. "Are we sure no one's under there?"

"Yep," Deputy Dawson answered then scratched at his belly hanging over his belt.

Where Reutgers was the department's future, Dawson was the epitome of everything wrong with the old regime. He was a coffee-guzzling, doughnut-popping chauvinist who reinforced the stereotype of *good ol' boy* law enforcement. On some days she wished his size thirteens would get in his way, tripping him up so he could retire with his pension and leave the real work to those who actually gave a shit.

"I'm not taking any chances. Call in Joyce and Armando. I want their dog out here, now." She crouched near the edge and drew in a deep breath. Under the damp, bitter scent of freshly turned earth and metallic rock, she tasted the burn of primer on the back of her tongue. It reminded her of the year she spent on the bomb squad during her anti-terrorism training.

Each night she had come home smelling like a fireworks factory. "Someone set this to blow."

Dawson snorted and tried to fold his arms across his chest, only succeeding as far as crossing his wrists. "Why would anyone go to the trouble to create a ditch with explosives?"

Her gut told her it had something to do with the tunnel found yesterday. "That's our job to find out. Bust out the gloves, boys. I want samples of dirt, rock and foliage from all over this area. I also want a geologist called out for a consultation." Oh what she wouldn't give for a proper forensic unit.

"A geologist? What for?"

"Unless you have a degree in topography or geology that I don't know about, I want to know what's so special about this stretch of rock."

He turned to spit then sucked at his teeth. "It'll just be a waste of time, and it's not like anyone was hurt."

"I'm sure these rangers appreciate your concern. If bending over is too much for you, Dawson, then find me the geologist."

"Where the hell am I going to find one of those?"

"It's called the internet. There are websites out there beyond the ones with three Xs in the URL. I want them in my office before noon."

"Fine." He turned away, muttering under his breath, "Sheriff needs to get laid."

Nope, problem was Sheriff got laid.

✦   ✦   ✦

AT 12:30 P.M. it was Reutgers who came through and had a professor from the University of Washington arrive in her office. His knowledge of the area, along with what she pulled from the permit office, gave her the first solid lead on a suspect and motive.

Eight miles over the ridge and down into the valley sprawled Neimi Gravel and Mining. Brett arrived just as the morning and evening shifts converged and parted ways. A female driving a squad car attracted a lot of lingering glances and a few wolf whistles, which she ignored as par for the course. This might have been the bosom of mother nature but it was also definitely man's land.

The stench of diesel fuel obliterated the sweet pine air and burned the inside of her nose. Before her lay a vast expanse of destroyed earth that stretched along the valley floor. The terraced steps of the giant pit looked like a street-whore version of the Grand Canyon. A fleet of dump trucks zig-zagged to the bottom and delivered their load to a hopper-type machine that ground its food into tiny bits and flushed it out onto massive conveyors headed for God only knew where. Gravel was the mine's bread and butter, but they recently entered the copper game, and the crash course she received from the professor an hour before hadn't prepared her for the reality of the destruction that fueled the modern world.

That's it, mandatory recycling of everything at the station. Fuck that, all of Cedar, she decided, closing her eyes to block the view of the wasteland below.

"Sheriff Briggs, what a surprise."

Brett turned to see Jebadiah Neimi approaching from the steps of a trailer. He wore a yellow hard hat and a matching vest. As one of Cedar's city council members, she had many run-ins with the head of Neimi Mining. His smooth charm and too-loud laughter always flipped on her bullshit meter.

"Aren't I a lucky man to have your beauty brighten what had been an unremarkable day."

Years of practice kept her pleasant smile in place in the face of such crap. She shook the offered hand just long enough to be polite and with the right amount of pressure to suggest that she wasn't a pushover to the Y chromosome. His hands were rough and gnarled, like a man who spent long hours doing manual labor. However, years spent behind the desk softened any other existence of a once fit body.

"So to what do I owe this pleasure?" he asked.

"I'm doing some research that I hope you can assist me with. Do you have a few minutes?"

"For a pretty lady? Of course. My office is this way."

He gestured for her to precede him back to the trailer and opened the door with a flourish. The darkened interior gave her pause as did the tightening pressure in her chest. Her hand instinctively hovered near her knife, her preferred weapon in close quarters, as she took the first step into the lion's den. The scent of wet rock and burned coffee blurred her vision, making it difficult to discern all of the maps and permits tacked to every inch of available wall space.

"Please, have a seat. Can I get you some coffee? I can close the blinds if it's too bright in here for you." He motioned to his face.

She sat gingerly on the edge of a metal folding chair and resettled the sunglasses, hiding her freakish eyes. "No, thank you. The light is fine. Just had my eyes dilated."

"What can I do for you?" Instead of taking a seat behind the desk, he sat on the corner by her knee.

A smile flirted with the corner of her lips at the subtle display of dominance. "I don't know if you've heard, but yesterday two children fell into a sinkhole in the national park."

"Oh, I've heard all about it. I'm sorry, Sheriff, but I don't know who he is."

She cocked her head. "He who?"

He reached for the newspaper lying on the desk then handed it to her.

The Chameleon Rescues Sheriff screamed the headline. The half-page photo captured a black-hooded Kristos as he jumped into the pit. His multicolored tunic blended into the scenery, obscuring most of his body.

Jiminy Christmas. They gave him a frickin' nickname.

The paper crackled like a dying firecracker in her tightening grip as she handed it back to Neimi. "No, I'm not here about…him."

"Any idea who he is? Did he really lift a two-ton boulder with his bare hands?"

"Unfortunately, I didn't get a good look." She shifted in her seat. "Mr. Neimi, I wanted to ask about what type of equipment is required to dig a tunnel."

He arched a blond brow. "What type of tunnel?"

"Oh, one about"—she stretched out her arms—"this wide and about four feet tall."

"What type of terrain are you digging through?"

"Mostly basalt."

His lips pursed in thought as he scratched his cheek. "Well, a good ol' hammer drill will get the job done, if you got nothing but time and years on your hands. But the most common tool is a continuous miner. It's a long, combine-type machine with a grinding log in the front that eats away at the rock."

"How difficult is it to obtain one of these machines?"

"Anyone with a decent cash flow can get a hold of one. If they're a small-end mine, renting would be a more viable option." He folded his arms and smiled. "Looking to get into mining, Sheriff?"

"Perhaps." She motioned to the window. "You've been in business here a while, haven't you?"

"Forty-five years," he said with pride. "We're the largest gravel provider in the state."

"I see you're tunneling as well as digging. Isn't that unusual for a copper mine?"

The light in his eyes dimmed as his smile turned from curious to shrewd. "Perhaps. But we aren't just mining copper."

"Really? Did you strike gold too?"

"Better than gold. Something really special." He stepped behind his desk and pulled open a drawer, withdrawing a spool of fine silver chain. "Do you know what this is?"

She leaned forward in her seat. "Not copper?"

He laughed and handed her the spool to examine. "This is molybdenite. This little mineral is used in all sorts of products, but mostly to strengthen other minerals. But science has discovered how to harness its strength all on its own. This little chain can hold fifteen tons. And if you mix it with carbon, it will burn longer and cleaner than any fuel in existence. Doing more with less material makes it a lot more valuable."

The chain was light in her hand and delicate enough to wear around the neck. She watched the light sparkle off the links as the end swung free and murmured, "So this is what you're mining for under the park."

He stared at her in surprise for a second before he leaned back in his chair with a chuckle. "No. That would be illegal."

She set the spool on the desk. "I would like to look in your mine, Mr. Neimi."

"Would you now? What for?"

"I want to look at these." She pulled a square piece of metal from her pocket.

"I don't know what that is."

"Sure you do. This is a plate that's screwed into the rock to keep the ceiling from crashing down. They're supposed to be spaced every few feet to maintain the integrity of the tunnel.

But in the one running under the park they were spaced too wide apart. I have a feeling your tunnels may have the same shoddy workmanship."

"You're a mining expert too?"

"No. But I have a friend who is."

He placed his hands behind his head with another laugh. "Sorry. Can't allow untrained civilians in the mine. Against OSHA rules. I'm sure you understand."

"Of course." She got to her feet with a small sigh. "I'll just call my friend and come back another day."

"Sheriff Briggs, did you know that I was great friends with your predecessor?"

Disquiet rolled from her stomach and lodged in her sternum again. "Is that so?"

"Yessiree. We were good friends. You could say we were partners. We worked together, helping each other make Cedar a productive, thriving community. I even got his grandson into Gonzaga. Paid for his education too."

A bitterness filled her mouth as if she'd taken a big gulp of the sludge in the coffee pot. "That was very generous of you."

"As I said, we were close friends. I helped him and he helped me." A speculative gleam entered his eyes. "Tell me about your goals, Sherriff. What is it that you most want?"

"I want to keep my town safe. Thank you for your time, Mr. Neimi. I'll be in touch."

His eyes raked over her in a gaze so lewd, the filth would take two showers to remove. "I'm looking forward to it."

Chapter Seven

"**Y**OU CALL THIS keeping a low profile?"

Kristos woke to his brother's bellow and the slap of a newspaper pegging him square in the face. He barely wiped the sleep out of his eyes before Lucian flipped the mattress, spilling him onto the floor.

"By the Gods, Luc. What is your problem?"

This was not how he was supposed to wake up the morning after a night of loving Brett. He was supposed to be in a warm bed next to his hot woman. Not tossed out of his bed just after falling asleep because he spent the previous night making sure said woman was not purposely running into danger.

He pulled the tangled sheet from over his head and frowned at the paper sprawled under his nose.

The Chameleon Saves Sheriff.

He stroked his chin and fluctuated between amused pride and embarrassed horror. If Brett saw this, she was going to have to get behind his brother in the kick Kristos' ass line.

"And you wore the royal armor?" Lucian continued to shout. "I swear, Kristosllanos, I wonder why I didn't leave you on the death stone."

"Don't blame me. I didn't come up with the name. I don't even know if I like it." He got to his feet and stretched his aching muscles. The day before had been more taxing on his body than a run down the river.

"You aren't listening to a word I'm saying. You—what is that?" Lucian pointed a shaking finger at Kristos' head.

Kristos went to look in the mirror above the dresser and sucked in a breath at the sight of his reflection. His two hearts kicked in exhilaration as he fingered the dark-blond lock that fell across his forehead. Brett's mark.

On Skandavia, when a man and woman gave each other to their keeping, their empathic abilities joined together so that they synchronized as true partners. When the bond was complete their hair and eye color changed to reflect the mated pair.

Brett let her fear stop the bond from completely forming, which is why the color leached from her irises instead of matching the jade-green of his. When the morning dawned and his appearance hadn't changed at all, he was half afraid he had completely misinterpreted her feelings for him. This little lock of gold confirmed what he knew all along. She belonged to him.

"You spoke the Vows of Eternity?" Lucian's voice raised an octave.

"Calm down." Kristos patted his brother's rigid jaw. "You'll have an aneurism."

He flicked at the blond lock. "I take it she rejected you?"

"Unless she speaks Skandavian, she doesn't know. That's why the bond is not complete." Kristos pulled a shirt and a pair of jeans from the dresser.

"What else?"

"She's stubborn."

"No." He shook his head and crossed his arms over his broad chest. "You did something. I can feel it on my skin like sandpaper. What did you do?"

Kristos scowled. With all of their abilities heightened on Earth, it was even more difficult to hide emotions he'd rather not have Lucian pick up on.

"I might have forbid her to work."

Lucian raised a brow. His lips twitched before he let loose with a deep chuckle, transforming his stern, drawn features into the charismatic man Kristos remembered. "You do have a suicide wish, don't you? The pride that woman has for her profession shines around her like a halo. It's her calling. She worked hard and made sacrifices to obtain her position. Did you think she would give it all up because of your profession of love?" When he didn't respond Lucian rolled his eyes. "Mercy take you, you did. It takes a strong woman to be mated to a *Llanos* and I've never thought of the sheriff as weak."

His spine snapped in indignation. "I know she's not weak. Brett is one of the strongest women I've ever known. She's brave, intelligent and has a warrior's spirit that not even half of our troops possessed. What that one tiny woman can accomplish frankly scares the shit out of me."

"Imagine the damage she could do if she knew our origins."

Kristos controlled his wince and continued to prepare for his shower, only to be pushed against the wall to face his brother's volcanic rage. "You told her!"

He pushed back against the solid wall of muscle. "Of course I did. She's my mate."

"Let me see if I understand." Lucian closed his eyes and pinched the bridge of his nose. "You have exposed your abilities to the public, fallen for a human who is the chief protector of her community, interfered with her duties, told her that you are an alien with superhuman powers, then forbade her from fulfilling her sworn oath after partially bonding with her."

"Maybe not in that order, but yes. Sit down before you hyperventilate." Kristos pushed his brother to sit on the bed. "Actually, she took the alien part very well. She was intrigued, compassionate. I sensed no fear from her. It couldn't have gone better, until she was called into work. Which reminds me, Brett's reaction to our origins is the least of our worries."

"Let me guess, you've scheduled a press conference as the Chameleon and are announcing that you are taking over the police force."

He wished, but Brett would have his balls in a vise if he dared suggest it. "No. Yesterday, when I was in that tunnel, I lost my powers."

Lucian turned statue still. "Explain."

"I don't know if I can. There I was, moving rock and dirt, forging a path to free Brett. The deeper I got, the more my muscles ached, my speed slowed. It was as if something was leaching away my strength. I felt human."

"Any other side effects?" Lucian jumped to his feet and began to pace. His movements reminded Kristos of the general Lucian once was. As Lucian paced, he tapped his finger against the tip of his nose.

"Just a lingering lethargy. It reminded me of that four-day training exercise over the Tulitian Mountains, when every man in the corps wanted you dead for pushing our bodies beyond all limits. No one was able to move without wincing for at least a week."

His eyes lit up with the memory. "When did your strength return?"

"As soon I climbed out of that hole. I wasn't back to normal, but significantly better."

"There must be something there, a mineral or plant life that affects our powers," he mused out loud. "What is this tunnel used for?"

"That's one of the issues. It's not supposed to be there. The national park is a protected area. It was pure misfortune that those adolescents were there when the roof collapsed. There was another cave-in this morning a quarter of a mile away but along the same path. I followed Brett to the site. She suspects that someone is hiding something. Once she made it safely to the station I came back here."

"I'll do some research on the geology of the area, collect some specimens." Lucian strode toward the door with an energy in each long-legged stride Kristos hadn't seen since they fought the Revolutionaries. He stopped in the doorway and turned back with a pointed finger. "I have not forgotten about your actions. I forbid you from donning the royal armor again."

Kristos scoffed. As if he would allow himself to be treated like a child. "You forbid me?"

"You do everything you can to prevent Brett from confronting danger because you say you love her. Well, you are my brother and I love you. I will not allow you to continue on this path that will lead to nothing but our destruction. If you want this woman so badly, go to her, talk to her, but this Chameleon nonsense ends now." He lowered his head and his green eyes glowed with a warning that once made entire armies fall to their knees. "If she doesn't stop you, I will."

Chapter Eight

B RETT STEPPED INTO the station and stopped short as the overwhelming stench of cheap perfume filled her nostrils. She took several halting steps toward her receptionist's desk and asked quietly, "Who's here?"

Janice snuck a quick glance toward the partially opened office door and whispered, "Council members Schmidt, Meeker and Mrs. Dubois."

Fan-fucking-tastic. "In ten minutes I want you to come into my office and declare a national emergency, got it?"

"Yes ma'am." The older woman covered her mouth and giggled as her eyes danced behind her bifocals.

Brett opened the door and strode boldly into her office. "Good afternoon. I thought the next council meeting wasn't for another week."

Milton Schmidt got to his feet and pulled on the cuffs of his suit and smoothed back his lacquered salt-and-pepper hair. "Hello, Sheriff. No, you're correct about the next meeting. We're here on a different matter."

She said nothing and closed the door. Clarice Dubois sat in Brett's chair behind her desk, stinking up the upholstery.

"Excuse me, Clarice, but I believe you'll be more comfortable over there."

Clarice raised an over-plucked brow, but sulked to the armchair on the other side of the office. "Sheriff, you must tell me your secret on how you manage to keep your hair so flat. I have such trouble taming my full tresses." She patted the helmet of bleached-blonde hair that curled around her shoulders.

Brett ignored the childish dig and looked back at the men. "How might I assist you?"

Schmidt and Meeker shared a look that put her immediately on guard.

"We received a call from Jebadiah Neimi," Schmidt answered. "He doesn't like the aspersions you've been making on his character."

"And what are those, exactly?" she asked.

Meeker cleared his throat and pulled at his long, gray beard. "He said that you're accusing him of a crime."

She pinched her lips into a tight line and nodded. "Mr. Neimi is indeed a person of interest and I treated him like I do any other suspect."

"And what crime are you accusing him of?"

"I can't discuss details of an open investigation. But I can say that I didn't go disturb the man because I don't have anything better to do."

The men shared another look while Clarice whipped out an emery board and started in on her thick, acrylic nails.

Meeker furrowed his brow and nodded to Schmidt, egging him on.

"Sheriff, Jebadiah Neimi is a respected member of this community. I'm sure that this is all just a big misunderstanding."

That same tingle of ickiness she felt in Neimi's office snaked down her back. "What are you saying, Mr. Schmidt?"

He raised his hands in a silent plea. "Let's forget about Jebadiah and concentrate on something more productive, like the Founder's Day festival."

The fucking Founder's Day Festival?

She forced down the curse that rumbled in her throat and took a step forward. The smile that curled her lip was pure honey as she slowly reached up and removed her sunglasses to reveal a narrowed, white-eyed glare.

Schmidt and Meeker jumped back with a gasp that was almost comical.

"You hired me to protect this community, did you not?" she asked in a low, deep voice.

Schmidt recovered first. "Yes, but we also hired you because we knew you would understand that we need to protect our friends as well."

"That's the second time today that I've heard the word friend and it sounded filthy. I'm well aware of what my job is and it's not to play favorites. Anyone who commits a crime will be arrested, no matter who it is. If I catch any of you so much as crossing a street against the big red hand, I will ticket you at the maximum fine. And if you try to stop me, I will arrest you for obstruction of justice. Am I clear?"

"Sheriff," Schmidt choked, trying to laugh off her warning while Meeker whimpered and tugged at his suspenders. No wonder Neimi had them by the short and curlies. "We aren't suggesting you bend the rules."

"Could've fooled me. What would you call it?"

"Excuse me, Sheriff," Janice poked her head around the door. "There's an emergency and you're needed immediately."

"One second, Janice. Gentlemen, Mrs. Dubois, I think this conversation is over. You know where I stand. And I know where you stand. Now if you'll excuse me, I have a job to do."

She marched out of the room with her head high and morals firmly intact. Her ego was a bit battered at the realization that she hadn't been hired for ability but her supposed malleability. Ha! The joke was on them. They hired a real sheriff so they could kiss her ass.

"Thanks, Janice. I owe you a coffee."

"Sheriff." She stopped Brett with an anxious grip on her sleeve. "I wasn't making that up. There's been a landslide in Harper's Ravine. It's blocking the river and the banks have been breached."

"It's blocking the entire river?"

"Yes ma'am."

"Tell them I'm on my way."

She raced out of the station and jumped into her car. Pressing the pedal to the floorboard, she sent the Crown Vic soaring over a hump in the road and landed with a teeth-jarring bounce.

With the river blocked, more than their little community would be affected. Along the banks lay dairy farms, fields of hops and barley, and towns like Cedar that would be washed away with a sudden deluge of water and debris if the pressure behind the blockade grew too great and was released too quickly. Upstream lay prime logging country and the mill that employed over half the town. But Brett's biggest concern was the Old Saw Bridge, so named for the crisscross pattern of antique two-man saws that decorated the railings. The bridge sat in the middle of Harper's Ravine, and with rush hour approaching, it would be teeming with vehicles.

She spotted Collins, Dawson and two other deputies at the scenic pullout over the river. She threw the car in park, but left the engine running as she raced to the edge of the ravine. "How's it looking?"

"Like God took a big piss," Dawson answered.

"Thank you for the visual."

A half a mile to her left was the twisted mess of rock, trees and dirt that formed the crude dam. Her brow furrowed as she followed the line of destruction over the ridge and into the forest. Unless she was mistaken, it was the same path the tunnel and cave-ins ran along.

At this part of the ravine the river reached ten feet down and spanned twenty yards. The dirty water batted against the dam, swirling and churning like a frothy milk shake. The backwash tore at the surrounding hillside as the downhill rush fought for dominance.

On her right, the Old Saw Bridge shook under the force of opposing currents. Water splashed up the sides and licked the undercarriage, ready to make a meal of the wood structure and appetizers of automobiles traversing along the top.

"Jesus," Brett cursed. "Why isn't the bridge closed?"

"We were waiting for you," Collins answered.

Her eyes popped out of their sockets. "If it's a choice between waiting for me or death, I choose not death for everyone."

"Look, it's the Chameleon," Deputy Joyce called out. She pulled a tube from her pocket and slicked on a layer of lip gloss then smoothed out the wrinkles in her coat. "Man, look at him go."

Brett leaned over the retaining wall to catch a better glimpse of the man in blue jeans and a black hoodie, racing down the hillside. He scrambled along the top of the makeshift dam and began clearing the largest boulders from the center. Her heart swelled and lodged in her throat as a tree trunk broke loose and came crashing straight for his head. He looked up and swatted it away like a volleyball, sending it soaring across the water to land with a huge splash.

"Who is he and can I get his number?" Joyce purred.

The deputies crowded around Brett, jockeying for the best spot to witness the spectacle.

"Crazy son of a bitch," she cried and spun to face the

group of men and one woman standing with their mouths hanging open. "Collins, Jaeger. Get down there and close that bridge. Dawson, Joyce. Call the city. I want a front-end loader at that dam, now."

"Where are you going?" Dawson asked as she jumped into her car.

"To stop that crazy ass from getting killed."

The car's engine caught with a roar as she pressed on the gas and tore off down the road. Tires squealed as she left the asphalt for a dirt trail usually used by meth runners, pot smokers and ATVs. Her teeth clashed together at a particularly rough bump, but she kept the pedal pressed to the floor.

What was Kristos thinking? He was a royal bodyguard and a river rat for Pete's sake, not a civil engineer or Superman. If the trees didn't crush him, then the water would suck him down to his death.

"You can't go, Brett," she mimicked his low baritone. "You'll endanger yourself and leave me all on my lonesome. Mother fucker. What do you call this? It's all right for you to risk your life, but not me?"

Sweat poured in her eyes and she flung the sunglasses away to better see the sun-dappled lane. More sweat gathered in her palms, making them slippery on the steering wheel.

Was this terrifying fear for his safety simply compassion for the welfare of another person, or was the thought of a future without Kristos too devastating to imagine?

So what if he was from another planet? He possessed most

of the important human body parts, some more impressive than others. His view on a woman's role in a relationship needed some serious readjustments, but he did genuinely care for her. Could she risk her heart, and his, by answering the plea in his jade-green eyes?

Ah, crap. You fell in love with him.

Denying the truth was useless. The man could sense her emotions so what good did it do to refute them? She may be in love with him but that didn't mean he had all of the power. Once this was over, she was going to have a nice sit-down chat with Mr. He-man. What was good for the goose was going to be branded on the gander with a hot iron if they were to have any type of relationship.

Up ahead the lane dropped off to where the Cedar River cut into the ravine. Brett hit the brakes and turned the wheel hard to the right. Rubber flew in all directions as smoke and dirt spewed from the tires on the passenger side of the cruiser. Metal grated on rock as she skidded toward the cliff in a frame-by-frame slide show until the ground gave way to nothingness. Her entire body locked in place and she closed her eyes tight as the back end of the sedan slipped over the edge.

A vision of Kristos' devilish smile was the last thing remembered as she wailed, "Son of a bitch!"

Suddenly, the car jerked from its downward momentum, her seat belt tightening across her torso. Her eyes flew opened and, as if she conjured him from a dream, she saw Kristos through the dirt-streaked windshield. The muscles in his arms strained as he gripped the car's bumper. His lips pulled back on a snarl as he dragged the two-ton machine back onto flat terrain.

The entire universe faded away as Brett sat in shock. Her fingers remained curled around the steering wheel and her eyes dried out from the inability to blink. Her lips tried to move, but her brain refused to function. Every synapse was a scrambled mess.

She was saved? How could that be? The car was going over the edge. She had been looking up at the overcast sky. She was supposed to be dead or at least severely jacked up.

Kristos ran to her door and yanked it so hard it came off the hinges with a metallic shriek. He snapped the seat belt out of the console and hauled her into his arms with so much force she knew he left bruises.

"By the Gods, Brett, I thought I wouldn't make it." She barely heard him over the roar of blood racing in her ears. "I thought you were gone." He peppered her face and hair with kisses. His big hands tracked down her back and sides then up to cup her face. "My *alskata*."

His blazing kiss began the slow thaw of her brain functions. Spiked with terror and relief, his lips and tongue reawakened her nerve endings and jolted her to consciousness. She melted into the kiss, breathing in his scent and the sting of cold mountain air. Her hands curled in his shirt, absorbing the solid strength of his pounding chest under her palms.

She pulled away with a gasp. "Oh God, what happened?"

He smoothed the hair that escaped her braid. "I felt your distress and came running, but then it spiked to terror." He buried his face in her neck and muttered a litany of words she didn't understand.

Despite the radiant heat of his body, her teeth chattered. Adrenaline heightened all of her senses. The crisp air, filled with the heavy scent of wet dirt and smoke, choked her, and the brilliant blue of his shirt was blinding.

Blue shirt.

"I don't understand," she murmured and ran her hands over the electric-blue cotton, shaking her head in confusion. "How did you know where I was?"

"I followed you from the lookout."

"No. You were down in the ravine, unblocking the river."

He frowned as well and traced his thumb over her eyebrow. "What? Why is the river blocked?"

"There was a landslide and it's causing the river to flood. You know that because you ran down to dig it out." He continued to stare at her as if the near-death experience was causing her to hallucinate. "If you're here then who is down there with a black hoodie covering their head?"

Kristos began to shake his head then his eyes widened with recognition. "Lucian."

The world spun as he scooped her into his arms and raced toward the landslide. His stride was fast like a cheetah, his gait smooth and steady, yet she clung to his shoulders so tightly her fingers ached. "Kristos, what's going on?"

"I'll explain later, I promise. But Lucian could be in trouble if he's near the earth."

They neared the edge of the crumbling ravine with caution. Kristos set her on her feet and motioned her to step out first. Lucian had created several small furrows that allowed the river to run through like a colander. Despite his efforts, the water continued to rise, covering the bridge until only the railings stuck above the surface.

She scanned the hillside for any spectators then turned back to wave the all clear at Kristos. "Get him out of there."

"Lucianllanos," he called and began to speak that melodic language she guessed was Skandavian. He flashed signals with his hands that made Lucian shake his head with each gesture.

A flash of yellow and a blaring horn brought her attention to the bridge up stream. A school bus sputtered mid-span, fishtailing in the deep water. The wood rail snapped like matchsticks as the bus crashed through the barrier. The rear tire snagged a piling, barely keeping the vehicle in place. The front bobbed like a fishing lure in time with the current.

"Goddammit," she shouted into the radio at her shoulder. "Why is that bus on the bridge?"

"Sorry, Sheriff. It was halfway across before we got here."

"Not good enough. Call in the paramedics and get out there now."

She felt the sizzle of electricity as the brothers shared a glance. Before she could blink, Lucian was off, skimming the rim of the ravine like a marble on a roulette wheel. Water sprayed behind him as he raced across the bridge and hauled the bus off the edge. Wrapping one arm around the remnants of the guardrail to use as an anchor, he began the slow crawl back to firm ground.

Little hands and faces stuck out from the bus's windows as the children clamored to see the hooded man in action. Imminent peril didn't appear to faze them as they jumped up and down and pumped their fists in cheer, while every adult in the vicinity watched with hands clenched together or covering their mouths, failing to see the thrill.

The moment Lucian set the bus on the bank the door slid open, spilling two dozen elementary students and one trembling bus driver onto the mud.

Kristos ran down to take Lucian's place at the blockade, which left Brett wearing a track in the grass as she paced back and forth with an eye on both brothers. This was wrong, all wrong. She was not supposed to play night watchman as two civilians risked it all. It was a bitter pill to swallow but if the brothers had not been there, lives would have been lost.

Brett reached for her radio. "That bridge stays closed until we get an engineer to look at it."

"Right, Sheriff," Collins answered.

"What's the ETA on that front loader?"

"It's approaching now. Maybe five minutes out."

"10-4." She cupped her hands around her mouth. "Kristos. The tractor is here."

He peered up at her through his drenched bangs and nodded, then kicked one last boulder out of the way. Water poured out like a cork popped from a keg. He traced to her side and grabbed her hand.

"No." She shoved him toward the trees. "I need to be here. Go, before you're seen and someone recognizes you."

"I'm not leaving you behind. I'll be close."

She cracked a grin. "I know. Just go."

Kristos might have physically left but his heat lingered like another layer of down in her coat. The weight of his gaze followed her every step as she waved at the driver of the front loader when he came into view.

Once she was convinced he knew how to safely drain the river's excess, she radioed dispatch. "Unit one to dispatch."

"Go ahead, unit one."

"My cruiser blew two tires and I'm in need of assistance. Please send a wrecker to the east side of Harper's Ravine. I'm about a half mile north of the Old Saw Bridge."

"Do you need medical assistance?"

"No, just the wrecker will do. And please notify the shop to have tires on standby for me." She grimaced. "And a new door."

"10-oh, uh, 10-4."

Brett cringed and rubbed at her temples. In five seconds half the force was going to know she wrecked her cruiser, and thirty seconds after that the rest would find out as well. Thankfully no one was witness to the particulars so she could make up a whopper of a tail to explain the damage.

Perhaps a bear that came out of nowhere, she mused, or she ran over a secret stash of meth supplies that was unfortunately lost over the cliff and into the raging river. Right, that...might work.

"Brett."

She turned to see Kristos standing tall and imposing at the edge of the woods. The fierce expression that tightened his mouth and clenched his jaw made her take a step back in surprise. "Kristos. What is it?"

"Come here."

The menacing rumble in the deep command straightened her spine as a dark streak of lust shot straight to her clit and made her pussy clench. Dammit, she hated how her body jumped to do his bidding.

She ignored the pull and rested her hand on her belt. "What is it?"

"Come here." He held out a firm hand. "Come to me."

"Oh please." She rolled her eyes. "Whatever little chauvinistic game you're playing at, Kristos, I don't have time. I have a job to do."

"Not now."

Before she could blink, his image blurred as he raced toward her and scooped her up his arms then headed deeper into the forest. She held back a shout and clenched fistfuls of his hair as the world streaked by in browns and greens. Where he was taking them, she hadn't a clue, but one thing was certain, he ran with purpose. Once they reached their destination, the tempest brewing in his jade eyes was going to unleash. The only question remaining was how she was going to weather the storm.

Chapter Nine

CRISIS HAD BEEN averted, yet the adrenaline bolting through his veins would not abate. His entire focus was on the woman in his arms and the bond that had not been completed. A fact that made his cock hard and balls ache in demand to take what was his and not waste another second.

She made not a sound as he hurtled over fallen trees and prickly shrubs. Her nails cut sharply into his neck where she held on tight but otherwise she gave no indication of her distress. Her courage and strength were tempered in the finest steel and that pissed him off to no end.

Brett was his, dammit. His to love. His to protect. And he nearly failed her. She was supposed to turn to him, rely on him for guidance and support. If he couldn't give her that, why would she want him?

His powers did not lend themselves to mind reading, an ability he would give his left arm for at the moment, but his empathic abilities picked up the intricate web of Brett's emotions. Relief at skirting death and the town being saved wove together with her worry for the safety of her men and areas of the river that had been affected. Combined with that was the subtle sweetness of her curiosity at his actions. At this moment in time he needed her to be thinking only of him and her lack of full attention was interfering with his ability to reason. Was it selfish? He didn't give a fuck. Brett was his world and his world had been threatened.

The fear he carried that she would be taken from him would not ease until he felt her life force surrounding him. He needed to feel the heat of her body, feel her heart beat strong against his hand while the rippling muscles of her cunt sucked at his cock. He needed to feel her alive in his arms and thinking of nothing but the pleasure he gave her.

"Kristos. Put me down, please," Brett requested in a soft voice.

"Soon," he promised and kept running until he reached a crowded cluster of hemlock trees.

A millions times he had dreamed of bringing Brett to this hidden place near the falls. The view of the river and the valley below was spectacular. The branches way up high provided protection from the rain and sun while the trunks offered privacy. As if privacy was a matter of importance. Soon he'd have Brett screaming so loud her cries would carry over the rushing water and echo across the hillside.

"Kristos, enough." Brett smacked his chest as he slowed his pace and set her on her feet. "You have to take—"

He cut her off with a hard kiss. He knew his little hellcat well. She couldn't deny him if her mouth was full of his tongue. He pressed her back against a tree and leaned forward in an attempt to imprint his body along hers. His lips and teeth ate at hers, desperate to assuage the ache in his chest. Brett pushed at his shoulders as her lips opened and her tongue tangled with his, giving him leave to take his fill of her. This conflict of her desires gave him the tether he needed to pull her to his thinking.

She wrenched her mouth away with a cry and pulled his hair when he dove in for another taste. With each deep lungful of air her breasts pressed into his chest, enticing him with the hard points of her nipples. "No. Stop. I can't breathe."

"No stopping."

She pulled his hair again and gasped, "Stop, Kristos. This is crazy. Take me back."

"No way in hell."

"My men need me."

"No," he roared. "*I* need you. You don't know. You don't know, Brett." His hands shook as he grasped her face between his palms. "You didn't see your car go over that cliff. You didn't see the look, the fear on your face as you thought you were about to die. I almost lost you. I can't lose you. Do you understand? You are my everything."

"Kristos," she whispered and stroked her fingers over the backs of his hands.

A sliver of her warmth snuck through the bars of icy fear that held him in its prison. It calmed him for all of a second until he looked down into her white eyes. Her lips were swollen and a pink flush graced her cheeks. Her eyes sparkled and were half-lidded with desire, but the iris was white. She had given a part of herself to him, but not all. Even after the events of the afternoon, she still kept her heart away from him. How could she not give in to the fire between them? How could she even think about walking away? She belonged to *him*.

Anger at her denial to accept all of him curled his lip and added fuel to the desire to replace her every thought with ones of him. His next kiss stole what little breath she had regained and offered no chance for refusal. He pushed the bulky sheriff's coat that kept him from her curves off her shoulders then reached for the belt at her waist. He needed inside her. Now.

Their heavy breathing formed clouds around their heads as the temperature dropped. Under his palms the skin of her hips was warm to the touch. He craved more of that heat and cursed the cloth that kept him from it.

He spun Brett around, pitching her forward. Her hands reached out for the scratchy tree trunk and kept them from tumbling over.

"Kristos. Please."

"I am going to please you." He nuzzled the tender crook of her neck and nipped sharply at her lobe. Her back arched, pressing her breast into his waiting hand. "That's all I want to give you, *alskata*. Pleasure."

He found her nipple beneath the fabric of her shirt and twisted, reveling in the spear of lust that lanced through her. His other hand unzipped her pants and slid along her belly to delve between her thighs. His cold fingers parted her folds and were immediately engulfed in the slick heat of her desire. Not even during the harshest of Skandavian winters did he remember being so cold, but then never had he feared for anyone like he did Brett. The hot evidence of her arousal brought to his awareness just how bleak and barren life would be without her.

"By the Gods, Brett." He bit at her neck. "Do you have any idea how good you feel?" He pressed two fingers deep into her sheath, searching for more of that wonderful heat. She hissed and bucked at the icy invasion. Her low moan and the rush of juice that wept from her pussy soothed any apprehension he might have had about pushing her where she didn't want to go. "You're like molten satin in my hand. I could bathe in your cream. Immerse myself in you until I drown."

He continued to fuck his fingers into her, twisting his wrist and grinding his hand against her plump clit. The scrape of her nails in the rough bark of the tree sent streaks of electricity down his back. He let go of her breast just long enough to free his cock from the stranglehold of his jeans. The shiny head throbbed a deep purple and pre-cum dribbled from the slit. Never before had he been so hard, so swollen that he could come from the mere brush of the cool breeze against his heated flesh. Where his fingers had been like ice, his dick was a flaming torch that could only be doused in the wet clench of Brett's body.

Pulling his fingers from her cunt, he hitched a breath as his cock notched at her opening. His thighs tensed to thrust.

"Wait," she shouted and flinched away. "Condom."

"No." The thought made his vision go red. He pressed his lips to her ear and growled. "Nothing will come between us. Nothing."

He drove his hips forward, withdrew and lunged again, pushing deeper and deeper until the mist-cooled curve of her ass pressed into his pelvis. With a roar he set a pace that made his teeth rattle and Brett's knees go weak. He caught her as she collapsed, taking them to the pine needle-strewn ground.

"So fucking good," he groaned, ramming harder. His fingers returned to her clit while his other arm wrapped across her chest, anchoring Brett, until he surrounded her as much as her pussy did him.

This was why he chose banishment, why he chose to live. For this moment in time when he lost himself in his lover's body, mindless to all but the fist-tight grip around his cock and her sweet cries dancing with the wind. How dare she deny him this moment with her independence and insecurity? He curled around her, determined to imprint himself upon her soul. Before the sun set there would be no doubt where his heart lay.

"You belong to me, *alskata*. In all ways. You know this." His eyes crossed as her inner muscles clenched tighter. "I'm going to come inside you. Fill you with my cum because you're mine. Every day, Brett. I'm going to come inside you every day so you'll always feel me in you."

Brett turned her head, using his biceps to muffle the screams that tore from her throat as her body shook and turned liquid beneath him. The sharp edge of her teeth in his flesh cut the thin thread leashing his control. Lightning streaked down his spine to detonate the dam that had built in his balls. Spots sparked before his eyes and it felt as if he were entering Earth's atmosphere again, the way he was torn asunder to be reformed into something new. He sensed the same connection and wonder in Brett as her pussy greedily soaked up the torrents of cum that spilled from his cock.

This is what he gave her that no one else could. Passion. Lust. Intense pleasure. And if she let him, his love. He was not going to lose her. Not to death and not to her own stubbornness.

They collapsed as one, chest's heaving and limbs twitching with the last of their release. His fingers curled, cupping her curves to gather her closer. "Mine. Always."

Chapter Ten

WELL...FUCK.

How much time had passed? Minutes? Hours? Brett never believed that one could pass out from orgasm. Leave it to Kristos to prove her wrong.

Her throat burned and her head swam as if she guzzled an entire glass of cheap whiskey. Tremors ran down her spine and along limbs still trapped in Kristos' embrace and her pussy continued to pulse in the most delicious way. Under the right circumstances, she might have enjoyed the sensations, but lying on the ground with a million pine needles sticking into her most delicate areas was not among them.

Frustration simmered in tandem with residual arousal. After staring death in its sinister face, she craved the connection that came with a good round of life-affirming sex and had been looking forward to falling into the oblivion Kristos created with his kiss and touch. After her shift was over.

She was sheriff. Always. Let him whip out his dick of temptation whenever he wanted, the badge came first. If he wanted a relationship with her, he had to respect the title.

Her laugh was as shaky as her arms as she tried to crawl

out from under two-hundred-thirty pounds of jackass. Even her fingers trembled with lingering orgasm. Relationship? Dictatorship was more like it. With Kristos it was his way or his way. Did he really think this caveman behavior flipped her switch? Well, on some levels it did, but disregarding her wishes was a sure-fire way to piss her off. He may be bigger and stronger, but she did have a brain and was quite adept at taking care of herself. The past two days were a complete anomaly.

"Stay." Kristos cupped her breast. "Let me share your warmth for a few more seconds."

"Don't start, Kilsgaard." She shoved off his touch and wobbled to a stand. A rush of liquid spilled down her thighs, reigniting her passion.

Getting angry at Kristos for taking her without a condom would be so easy, but damn his bare cock had felt so good sliding deep. Just the memory of the way he had grown hot and hard before jerking with his release was enough to make her come again. It had been in her power to stop him had she really wanted to. He was strong but a Taser made for one hell of an argument. The elixir of body fluid was more female than male, if she were honest. But Kristos didn't need to know that.

She cinched her belt one notch tighter than normal and mentally gathered the fragments of her scattered conscience. First priority was to contact her men and make sure they weren't beating the bushes looking for her.

She spotted her radio near the base of the tree. God, she

hoped it hadn't turned on and broadcasted her screams to the world. A breath eased from her lips when she saw the switch was firmly to the off side. She flipped it on and raised the mic to her lips. "Unit One to Unit Four, come in."

"What are you doing?" Kristos asked, using his hands to awkwardly struggle into a stand.

She smirked at his sex-drunk movements. "Damage control."

Collins answered her call. "Unit Four. Heard you had some car trouble, Sherriff. You okay?"

"I'm fine. The tires aren't so good. The river is looking better down here." She winced at the lie. "How's it on your end?"

"Still high but no longer rising. The Chameleon bought us valuable time."

Kristos raised a brow at that and crossed his arms over his inflated chest with a smug grin.

She turned her back to him. "Keep up the good work. I'll check in when the wrecker arrives. Over."

"Brett, where are you going?" Kristos called after her as she took off at a brisk march.

She had no idea where he had taken her but all she needed to do was keep the river on her left to return to the cruiser. How long would the car be out of commission before she could check the territories affected by the flooding?

"Brett, stop. *Alskata*, wait." He gripped her around the arm.

His touch broke through her mental concentration. She

turned on him with a snarl. "Don't *al*-whatever me. You've interfered enough with my job. And with me."

He hastened to keep up, tripping over his jeans. "You're job takes second place to your safety. I will not stand by and watch you risk your life. And if you're worried about becoming pregnant, don't be. Your hormones are tied to your emotions. You're angry but not pre-menstrual."

The absoluteness in his tone made her hand itch for her gun. She tried to tune out his stupidity and kept moving forward. They'd had this argument before and she refused to engage in a fruitless shouting match.

"I'm not kidding, Brett. Let someone else be sheriff. If you must work, help in the office, but you will stay out of danger."

She choked in outrage that he actually spouted such asinine words. "Oh my God. You really want me to punch you, don't you?

"I almost didn't reach you in time. Do you have any idea how I felt, what it did to me to have your life hanging by my fingertips? Do you even care?"

"Shut up! Just shut up." She swung to face him, gabbing fistfuls of his shirt and giving him a firm shake. "I know exactly how you feel. My father died while on duty and I had to watch my mother mourn him every day thereafter, so I am well aware of what it means to wear the badge. Do not make the mistake of thinking I'm oblivious to the pain." Her voice cracked. Furious tears sprang to her eyes, but she refused to give in to them. "When I thought Lucian was you and I saw that tree fall straight for you…" She paused to swallow. "For that split second I thought you were a goner and a part of me died. That's why I was driving so fast to stop you."

"Brett," he sighed and brushed the hair off her cheek with a gentle hand.

She turned her face from his touch. "No. Don't. Just because I understand how you feel does not make you right. Yes, I care about you. And yes, I know that there's a strong connection between us. But you do not get to disregard my wishes. I am sheriff and you have to respect that. If we are to have any future together you have to let me do my job. This stupid, bullshit, chauvinistic behavior pisses me off and makes me want to step on your balls until they explode, and I happen to like your balls, so shut up." She pointed to the cluster of trees behind them. "Pull another asshole stunt like that again and I will put on my heaviest boots and dance a salsa on your dick. Are we clear, Kilsgaard?"

Kristos sighed and looked away. His lips pinched with the argument she saw burning in his eyes. "I can't do that."

"Why? Because I'm a woman?"

"Yes."

A bolt of shock raced from the top of her head, down her sternum and froze her in place. Several long seconds passed where her brain tried to form a sentence, yet she could do nothing more than work her jaw up and down.

He grimaced and shook his head. "Brett, let me explain."

"No," she managed to squeak out. "I'm beginning to understand that where you come from the women are more docile and reliant on a man to take care of them. But here on Earth, especially in this country, women have something that's called freedom. I choose to be a cop because I'm good at it. I make a difference. Why are you so intent on changing who I am? Why am I not good—Never mind." She fought the tears stinging her eyes. "I'm done fighting with you. I'm so done."

Brett left Kristos with her heart in her throat. If he truly believed that a compromise was unattainable, then it was better to end whatever was between them now, before their connection grew stronger. As it was, the pain of walking away burned like a sticky bandage ripped slowly from her flesh. Any man who made her break her own rule on relationships needed to believe in her one hundred percent. She would not settle for less.

"Excuse me, Sheriff." Kristos caught up with her a hundred yards from where she left him staring after her. He matched her stride but made no move to touch her. "I'm sorry."

She didn't say anything. He may be sorry now but actions spoke louder than words.

"Let me carry you back."

"I can walk."

"You do know we're about five miles away from your car?"

Jiminy Christmas. Brett stopped and pinched the bridge of her nose. In through the nose. Out through the mouth. After a glare up at the gray sky she ordered, "Squat."

"What?"

"Squat down." She motioned with her hand. He bent down low enough for her to climb onto his back. "Take me straight to the car. If you deviate so much as a foot from that direction, I will kick you in the kidneys. Understand?"

He stifled a chuckle and wrapped his hands around her thighs to resettle her weight. "Aye, Sheriff. By the Gods, you are so violent."

"It seems to be the only thing that gets your attention. It must be your warrior blood."

"Your hot little pussy grinding against my spine gets my attention too—ouch!"

She let go of the chunk of hair she pulled. "Do not provoke me."

This time he laughed loud and hearty and gripped her tighter. The wind stung her eyes as he ran. His speed and agility amazed her, yet she didn't feel fear. Kristos would always see to her safety, whether she wanted him to or not.

Kristos took her directly to her vehicle. The torn tires and busted door sent a shiver of memory down her back.

In her arms, Kristos tensed as well. "You ask too much of me, *alskata*."

She tapped his shoulder and he set her on her feet. "I ask for you to have faith in me."

"In you, yes. The world? Not so much."

"Why do you want me, Kristos?"

He tilted his head and stared at her with those jade-green eyes as if waiting for her to say more. "I do not understand," he said.

"Of course you don't," she sighed. "Why do you want to be with me? What is it about me that's attractive to you?"

"Why do I feel like this is a trap?"

She smiled. "Answer the question. Please."

He sucked in a breath and rubbed his forefinger against his chin. "Well, besides your incredible beauty and innate sexiness." He grinned when she threw him a terse glare. "I'm drawn to your strength, your courage. The compassion you show to those around you is very attractive, as well as your intelligence. You prove yourself to be a mate who any man would be proud to have by his side, and who would be a good mother for his children. That is why I want you, Brett."

She hadn't been fishing for compliments, but the honesty in his words touched her on a level no man had before. One more chunk of the wall she kept between them crumbled at the same time her conviction of the beliefs she must hold on to strengthened.

"Then why are you trying so hard to change me?"

"I'm not. I only want you safe, Brett. I love you for who you are."

"But every time you spout that bullshit about being yours and how you won't allow me to do my job is an attempt to strip me of the very things you just claimed to like about me."

"That's not true."

"She's right."

Lucian appeared from out of the shade of an oak tree. His

cheeks were flushed and a light of excitement bounced in his eyes that she had never before seen from him.

"This doesn't concern you, Lucian." Kristos crossed his arms over his chest, subtly flexing the muscles of his pecs and biceps.

"However much I like watching you make an ass of yourself, I like the sheriff more. You do her a great disservice with your lack of respect."

Kristos' eyes flashed a bright green and his nostrils flared. "I do respect her. I've told you that many times."

"Then prove it. Quit trying to change her. She is not our queen."

"I know she's not!" Kristos shouted and took a menacing step toward his brother. "Stay out of this. It is none of your concern."

"I'm sorry, but when you make a public spectacle like the one you did earlier that upset half of the forest, you make it my concern."

"Lucian." She stepped between the brothers who appeared to grow larger with each heated exchange. Flames burned her cheeks at the thought of Lucian overhearing Kristos' rutting rampage. Lord, what he must think of her. Best not to dwell on it and change the subject quickly. "Thank you for saving those children. I don't like you putting yourself at risk like that but you have my gratitude."

He glared at his brother for a long minute before bowing slightly at the waist. "You are most welcome. I know if you had the time and manpower you would have seen to their safety."

"Oh, by the Gods," Kristos groused and rolled his eyes.

Lucian gestured to her squad car. "What happened here?"

"I guess I hit a bump too hard and blew the tires." She crouched by the front tire for a closer inspection of the torn rubber. A slit in the sidewall caught her attention. As she probed the crack with her finger, a warning tingle gathered in her lower spine.

"What are you thinking?" Kristos hovered over her shoulder.

She bit her lip. "This looks odd." She crawled toward the rear tire and ran her fingers over the edge, her frown deepening when she found a matching gash.

"What is this?" Lucian pulled a length of chain that was wrapped loosely around the front license plate.

The tingle turned to burning outrage as her gaze narrowed on the four-foot-long chain dangling from Lucian's grasp. She pressed her lips tight together to hold back the volley of curses that would do nothing but set off Kristos' protector meter.

It didn't work. "Your anger just spiked like a volcanic eruption. What is it?"

She pointed her finger at him in a stern admonishment. "Don't sense my emotions."

"Brett, what is that?"

"Please, tell us," Lucian seconded. His gaze focused on the chain as his brow crinkled in confusion. He passed the chain from one hand to the other before holding it up to the weak sunlight to examine it from all angles.

"It's a chain."

"From…"

"I saw one similar in Jebadiah Neimi's office."

"As in Neimi Mine and Gravel?" Lucian asked, still toying with the chain as if it was the most fascinating object he had ever encountered.

"Yes."

Papa Bear stepped closer. "Why is it wrapped around the license plate?"

"I'm guessing that it's a warning. I had some questions for him about the cave-in. He showed me a length of chain similar to that made from a mineral called molybdenite. When heated just right it's supposed to be the strongest thing on the planet."

"And you suspect that he's mining for this mineral under the park?" Kristos asked her while watching Lucian with a frown that deepened with each graceful movement of his brother's hands.

"Yes." The curiosity finally broke her. "What are you doing?"

The corner of Lucian's lips curled. "I have some suspicions of my own."

"Care to share?" she asked when an explanation never came.

"When Kristos told me how he lost his powers in the cave I went to do a little investigation. After being underground for a few minutes, I began to feel weak, like after a grueling run up the mountain. I was about to gather some soil samples when the ground began to shake. I followed a maze of tunnels until I reached the surface and saw the land slide down to block the river. By then my powers had somewhat returned."

"And you feel that weakness now holding that chain?"

"I do," he said, more in wonder than concern. "However this is a bit different. A slow sucking of my energy as opposed to the overwhelming exhaustion I felt in the tunnel. I wonder."

He walked to the front of the cruiser and gripped the bumper with both hands. With a deep grunt, he lifted the front of the car. His arms shook and his lips pulled back over his teeth. Picking up a Crown Victoria was no small accomplishment, but from what she'd seen of the Kilsgaard brothers it should have been as easy as retrieving the morning paper.

The front bounced as he dropped it back on the ground. Sweat clung to his upper lip and his eyes appeared dazed. "Here, Sheriff, put this back in your pocket."

She tucked the chain away. "Are you all right?"

"We shall see. What concerns me now is that this man sabotaged your car."

"Right." She kicked at the remains of the tire in thought.

"Did you know," Kristos said, "that when I'm near a person who is worried I feel a sick, swirling sensation right behind my sternum and a there's a bitter taste on the back of my tongue, just like I can taste right now?"

She rubbed at the back of her neck. "Neimi may have insinuated that Sheriff Billings might have known about the digging and bought his silence." After her meeting with the three council members, she now knew it wasn't an insinuation. "If the sheriff was on the take, I have to wonder if one or more of my men are in on it and if it was one of them that sent the warning."

It was one thing to not have her men's respect because she was a woman, it was almost expected, but to have one of them out to do her harm cut deep. Your police brethren were supposed to have your back. It was one of those things that was unquestionable. Now who was she to trust?

"I need to get to my office."

"How can you think of returning when you have a target on your back?" Kristos exclaimed.

"Kristos." She fisted the front of his shirt and pulled him down until they were nose to nose. Whether it was his powers or some cosmic connection they shared, the rolling in her stomach was just like he described. She could taste his fear for her. "I understand your fear and I thank you for saving my life. I'll be careful. But you have to trust me. Please." She pressed her lips to his in a soft kiss that was a promise as well as a request. "Meet me at my house later. I know you can let yourself in."

He closed his eyes tight and a shudder rolled through his body. She stroked his chest, thankful that he was making an effort not to immediately overrun her wishes.

With a deep breath, he opened his eyes. "I have complete faith in you. But if I don't hear from you by midnight I'm coming after you."

She shook her head with a chuckle. It was a start.

As he trailed his finger over her cheek, it was then that she noticed the dark-blond lock of hair curling over his left eye. In all of the excitement she had completely forgotten about her eyes.

She wound the strands around her finger and let it go. "We have a lot to discuss."

At least he had the grace to blush. "If you need anything call me."

"I will." And she meant it.

"Ready, Lucian?"

"One moment." He gripped the bumper of the cruiser and lifted the front as high as his shoulders and set it back down as if it were a Matchbox toy.

"I think Lucian has found a new puzzle." He kissed her again. "Anything and I'm there."

She pushed at his chest. "Go."

They disappeared into the brush but she knew Kristos hadn't gone far. The fight with him for her independence was not going to be won with one battle. Patience was the key, and lord above, she hoped she had enough. But he was trying and his effort would not go unrewarded.

A flashing red light preceded the arrival of the wrecker trundling down the dirt road. Jerry stepped out with a whistle and wiped a red rag over his heavily lined forehead. "Wowie, Sheriff. God must've been watching out for you to keep from plunging over that edge."

Hysterical laughter flirted with her lips. "You could say that."

Chapter Eleven

I T WAS AFTER eleven when Brett ended the last of a long line of phone calls. In the Cedar Sheriff's Office, resources were slim and she wore many hats. When she left the city police she made sure she maintained connections with the right people. It might take a while before she had her answers but the ball was rolling. With nothing more to do but wait, she changed her into her civvies and headed home.

She opened the door to the soft sound of the *Late Show* on the television. After hanging up her coat, she crept into the living room and took a moment to enjoy the sight of a sleeping Kristos splayed out on the sofa. The light from the TV flickered over his face in blues and greens, making him look like an alien. One leg hung over the back of the sofa and the opposite hand rested on the floor. *He is so frickin' adorable,* she thought with a quirk of her lips.

He started when she turned off the television and sprang to his feet. "Hey." He ran his hands through his hair. "Welcome home."

He held open his arms and her feet barely touched the floor as she flew into his embrace. Strands of hair from her braid stuck in his stubble as he rubbed his cheek against the top of her head.

She had long ago forgiven him for his earlier behavior. Mostly. Once she was ensconced in the privacy of her office, and the crazy events of the last forty-eight hours had become nothing more than memories, she had been able to really focus on her feelings for Kristos and thought about what changes they would bring to her life. Their dilemma was not going to be solved overnight. Baby steps, it was going to take baby steps to prove to him she could be a superwoman and do it all. Withholding her affection would only her hurt as well as him, and after the stress of the day she needed his touch.

With a soft sigh, she snuggled deeper into his embrace.

"The night must have gone well. You feel so content."

"Nothing concrete but I have some feelers out." She hugged him tighter around the waist then pulled back to stand on her tiptoes. As her lashes drifted shut, she saw the slow curl of his smile before his lips touched hers.

A lazy river of heat seeped into her bones, melting away the tension caused by a rough day. The tip of his tongue skimmed along the seam of her lips and she opened without hesitation, coaxing him inside to taste his fill.

"Perfect," he whispered against her lips.

Pure joy. That was what letting go of old fears brought to her life, pure joy. It wrapped her in a fuzzy cocoon from head to toe and made her damn glad to be alive.

"I'm going to jump in the shower." She took his hand and

tugged him behind her. His deep chuckle sent shivers down the back of her neck and across her nipples. The tips beaded against the fabric of her sensible bra, scraping the delicate skin with a promise of what was to come.

The bathroom shrank in space the moment Kristos joined her. His hand brushed her backside as he turned the water on in the shower, while her own hand trailed slowly over his abdomen as she reached for a stack of towels.

He stopped her when she reached for the band tying back her hair. "Let me."

His fingers were gentle as he released the strands. He smoothed the ends over her shoulders and down her breasts. "Do you know how hot it makes me knowing that I'm the only man to see you this way?"

God, she hoped it was as hot as he made her.

His green eyes glowed brighter as she stripped the sheriff away to reveal the woman beneath. The woman who ached for her man. The desire in his gaze flared into stark hunger as she slid her trousers over her hips.

Steam swirled around his shoulders as he slowly undressed, returning the tease. She finally had to look at the floor and bite her lip to keep from giggling with unadulterated glee. This perfect creation of man was getting naked in her bathroom? Unbelievable.

"What's so funny?" he asked.

"Nothing."

"I can feel your laughter. It's like a billion bubbles racing over my skin."

She slapped at his arm. "Stop feeling my emotions. I hate that."

He shook his head and lifted her into the shower. "Can't be helped. We're connected, you and I."

"Connected, huh?" She leaned her head back into the spray. "Is that why my eyes are white?"

He suddenly took a deep interest in creating the perfect swirl of bath gel on his palm. "Perhaps."

"Explain, please."

"Now?" He slid his soapy hands over her breasts, massaging and squeezing the soft mounds and making her eyelids drop in pleasure. "You don't want to talk now."

"Yes, I do."

"Nah, not now."

She let out a soft moan as he twisted the tips, alternating the pressure and rhythm that kept her off-balance. He was good but she was not without her own tricks. She forced her eyes open and reached up to tug at the hair along his nape. "Now. I'm not going anywhere." She scraped her nails along his chest as her other hand cupped his balls. "And neither are you."

His groan rumbled down his body to where her fingers rolled and squeezed his sensitive sac. The vibration ran up her arm and set her clit to throbbing. It took a herculean effort to keep from dropping to her knees and taking his cock to the back of her throat. He tasted so good but she needed answers more than his flavor on her tongue.

"That's a very effective interrogation technique you've developed," he moaned. "They teach you that in cop school?"

She squeezed the base of his shaft. "Talk."

"You're evil." He kissed the tip of her nose then reached down to still her hand. "On Skandavia when a man and woman decide to join their lives together, one of them will speak the sacred bonding words while making love and their emotions intertwine. That way they will always know what the other is feeling no matter where they may be. Instead of exchanging jewelry they exchange physical traits to show that they've mated."

Realization cut through the sensual fog like a knife. "You spoke those words to me?"

His cheeks went red, and not from the hot water. "Yes."

"Are we...mated?"

"Not yet. Subconsciously you picked up on the bond and refused to complete the connection."

"How long does the bond last?" she asked, although she suspected his answer.

"'Til death us do part."

The shower stall seemed to close in around her. Hot air filled her lungs, suffocating her, as she struggled to take in a calming breath. He took her choice away from her and, what, she was supposed to be grateful? "How could you do that without asking me?"

"I'm sorry—No. Actually, I'm not." He cupped her face in

his hands. "I'm not sorry I said the words to you. If I thought for a moment that I was forcing you into something you didn't want then I'd feel guilty. I know you want me but you fight it. You have a fear of the future. I had hoped that once we bonded you would share my strength in us."

She shook her head, unable to face the passion and certainty in his eyes. "What makes you so sure of what I want?"

He placed his hand over her heart. "Because I *feel* you. I feel what's in your heart, what you fight."

Trapped in the circle of his brawny arms, she couldn't run from the truth. This was way beyond taking things one day at a time, enjoying the moment for what it was. Yes, she loved him, but how could she plan a future when there was a very real possibility there wouldn't be a future? The logic was insane, she knew that, but the fear lingered.

"Why am I here now, Brett? Have you stopped running?" Steam filled the room, obscuring her surroundings. In the white billowy clouds Kristos was an avenging angel claiming his earthly prize. He pressed the hard planes of his body to her soft curves, smoothing his hands down her spine to cup her buttocks. "I wish you'd show the same courage you use at work with me."

That was different. Wasn't it?

He didn't give her the chance to respond as his lips sealed over hers, incinerating any thought of denying him her passion. Perhaps more than their physical traits had been exchanged with the attempted bond. His hunger for her punched her in the chest, filling her with a fire that made her heart pound and her thighs slick with cream. Empty. God, she was so empty.

The tips of his fingers skirted along the cleft of her hind cheeks before he pressed two deep into her slick sheath, caressing the sensitive nerves and making her writhe. He swallowed her cry as he pushed his thumb into the untried passage of her backside.

"Do not tell me you don't love this." He panted against her cheek. "Dear Gods, you're melting in my hand."

Brett bit her lip until she tasted blood. The wicked pleasure was unbelievable. She was so wet, her pussy gushed as he worked her body to a fevered pitch of want. She wanted to come so badly, she wanted his cock filling her, she wanted his cum to splash inside. She wanted Kristos.

"I can feel you, *alskata*. I feel your desire, the way your heart pounds, the fire in your veins, the uncontrollable clench of this sweet pussy. It's so electrifying it burns in my belly and tightens my balls. It's almost as good as being inside you."

"Please, Kristos. Please," she begged, not sure what she cried out for. "I can't—I can't—" She squeezed her eyes shut as her knees gave out.

He was right there to catch her as she collapsed. He lifted her against the wall and impaled her on his pulsating cock, driving deep and true.

It was too much. Kristos was too much. His touch, his kiss, all overwhelmed her. Breathing was impossible as she drowned in a tidal wave of pleasure so intense her belly cramped and her muscles ached with effort to fight the all-consuming desire to let go, to unleash her fear and give her entire keeping to Kristos.

And he knew it. "Don't fight it. Don't fight me."

His powerful thrusts picked up speed, shuttling her to the edge of mindlessness. Her fingers slipped off his shoulders and her legs refused to grip his hips, but true to his nature, Kristos kept her secure in his grasp.

"It's too good." Her tears mingled with the spray from the shower. "It's too much."

"It's all that I am," he groaned then thrust so deep the head of his cock nestled deep in her core, jetting his hot seed and branding her as his.

Her screams echoed against the tile as the tornado of her orgasm picked her up and threw her into oblivion. Her mind was not her own. Her body writhed and convulsed in ecstasy, soaking in every drop he produced, as if her body was a desert and he the first rain.

"I love you, Brett," he murmured into her neck. "I love you."

He didn't need to say the words. She felt his emotion more keenly than she her own. His love for her was so beautiful, so bright and warm, like a bonfire on a cold night. It was sweet like the ripest berry, more dazzling than the biggest diamond. It amazed and humbled her that he felt so strongly for her, Brett Briggs. What had she done to deserve something so pure and amazing?

She continued to cry, overwhelmed by the flood of emotion. He kept her in his arms as he turned off the water and carried her out of the shower. Setting her on the counter, he pulled out a towel to rub her dry before focusing on himself.

While her tears ebbed, she watched him whisk the towel over his skin. He paused when he caught a glimpse of his reflection. Blond streaks ran through his hair like a tiger's pelt. She turned to look in the mirror. The irises of her eyes were still white. The bond was not complete.

"Kristos, I'm sorry."

He placed a finger over her lips. "I don't need the words, Brett. I know."

Son of a bitch. He made her want to cry again. She couldn't complete the bond. Not now. Until she put an end to whoever was threatening her, she couldn't make a promise to Kristos no matter how much she wanted to otherwise. Yet guilt about not saying that she loved him was there because she did, and he deserved someone who embraced that love wholeheartedly.

"Can I carry you to bed?"

She nodded, her voice raw from her screams and the love she didn't dare speak out loud.

As he carried her she didn't feel weak or helpless, but cherished. He wanted to take care of her. He wanted to see to her needs and now she understood that it didn't mean he didn't think her incapable. He loved her, and because of that, he wanted to do for her.

A techno-dance beat shrilled from the bathroom the moment he set her on the sheets. She pointed to the pile of clothes scattered across the threshold. "That's my phone."

"I'll get it."

He dug into the pocket of her pants and retrieved the phone, bringing it back to hand it to her. She was very impressed he didn't look at the display or say a word. She pressed the screen to see the text message waiting in the inbox. It was her contact from her former department.

Found a trail that's very promising. I'll call in a few hours.

"Do you have to go?" He sounded calm and half interested, but his body went tense and he held his breath.

"Nope, just getting the routine check-ins." She turned off the ringer then set the phone on the nightstand. She turned back around to kiss his lips.

"Good, then I get you all night long."

She rested her cheek against his chest and stared at her cell phone, waiting for Kristos to fall asleep.

✦　✦　✦

NOW THAT'S HOW a man should be woken up.

Kristos sighed and ran his fingers through the silky tresses of the woman sliding her tongue over his belly. "What time is it?"

"Dark," she answered in a voice still husky from her earlier screaming orgasm. "Your body heat is keeping me awake. If you plan on sleeping over here again, I'm gonna have to install an air conditioner."

"Done."

Her throaty laugh buzzed against his abdomen, shooting electricity to his rapidly hardening shaft. By the Gods she was magnificent. The soft moonlight turned her creamy skin alabaster and added silver highlights to the wavy hair that pooled across his chest. She had put on a lacy black bra and panty set that emphasized her luscious curves and scratched teasingly against his skin where she brushed against him.

Brett's passion was sweet and spicy, like warm mulberry wine. It poured over him in a hot wave that reminded him of sinking his cock into her tight pussy.

He tugged on her hair. "Ride me. Now."

She laughed again. "You're so bossy." She caught his hands and pressed a kiss into each palm then placed his hands over the lace-covered globes. "Do you like my breasts?"

"Silly question. Of course I do." He massaged and squeezed, giving her nipples a hard pinch. "Now ride me."

"I knew it was going to go down this way." From behind her hip she produced a shiny set of handcuffs and slapped one end around his wrist. "Don't make this difficult, Kilsgaard."

Intrigued by what she was planning in that pretty head of hers, Kristos allowed her to stretch his arms over his head and attach the cuff to his other wrist. The soft clang of chain against the metal bedframe sent goose bumps along his flesh. "What's this all about?"

"You're under arrest."

"For what?"

She squeezed the base of his cock, sending a bolt of pleasure to his balls that drew them tight with an ache to release. "Carrying a loaded weapon without a permit."

Their eyes met for several long moments before they both burst out laughing. She fell to her side and covered her face when her laughter turned into a snort.

"I can't believe you actually said that," he gasped when he could draw a breath.

She wiped a tear from her eye. "I can't either. I've never said that to a man in quite that way before."

"I should hope not. You're mine."

"Am I?" She hummed with a secret grin and smoothed her hands over his chest and down his legs. It was a leisurely perusal that had his hands clenching with the urge to break his bindings and pin her to the mattress. This playful side of Brett surprised him and made him realize he had so many wonderful things he had yet to discover about his woman. He'd let her have her way with him. Even if it killed him.

Her lips were petal soft and her tongue a hot, wet lash that seared his heated skin. As she trailed kisses along his inner thighs, the cool jade pendant around her neck grazed his cock with light, teasing flicks followed by the scratchy fabric of her bra. The contrast of texture and temperature twisted the coil of his desire until the metal bedframe dented in his grip.

She straddled his waist. The hot pad of her cunt teased him through the black lace. She pulled a lacy cup down to expose a puckered tip. "Suck my nipple."

"Yes ma'am."

No need to ask him twice. He pulled the pink bud into his mouth and rolled it against the roof of his mouth. The silky skin of her inner thighs brushed his sides as she wiggled and shimmied like a live wire. He buried his nose against her skin and took in her incredible scent, jasmine with a hint of cinnamon. She was intoxicating and it made his head spin.

The dizziness worsened until he had to close his eyes to concentrate on the beautiful woman kissing her way to his straining cock. With each breath his body sank deeper into the mattress. What magic was she weaving that made it seem as if he were floating between fantasy and reality?

Her nails scraped his flanks as her tongue danced a line from hip bone to hip bone. The sensation made him hiss in pleasure, but there was something wrong. It was as if the wick of their emotional connection was slowly being turned down until it sputtered out.

Kristos lifted his heavy eyelids and tried to shake the cobwebs from his mind. A glint of silver from the corner of his vision caught his attention.

While he had been preoccupied by Brett's drugging kisses, she had been busy wrapping a chain of molybdenite around his arms. He tugged against his bonds with nothing but a soft clink for his efforts.

"Brett." He tried to keep his rising panic from his voice. "What's this about?"

"I don't want you to escape and take control. This is my show."

"*Alskata—*" He groaned as she took his shaft deep into her mouth.

Without their emotional tether, all of the sensation was centered on the ache in his balls and throbbing beat in his cock. The sensation wasn't unpleasant but he missed feeling her in his mind as well as heart. Her hands worked in tandem with the edge of her teeth and the suction of her lips to bring him quickly to the edge.

"Brett, untie me. I promise I'll let you do whatever you wish. Let me go."

In response she tightened the suction of her mouth. The sight of her saliva, wet on his flesh, drew a whimper he was quick to squelch. From beneath her lashes, her pale eyes dared him to beg.

A *Llanos* never begged.

Her smile grew wider with the challenge and her moan of approval vibrated down his length and up his spine. His fierce warrior was as wicked in the bedroom as she was in uniform. Why he thought she would give any quarter was a mistake born of his male ego. He didn't need their connection to know she was going to work him over like a prize fighter in the ring.

As his eyes rolled back into his head he figured it was a lesson he might be willing to relearn again and again.

The backs of her knuckles skimmed under his sac then lower. When she speared her finger deep into his ass, he couldn't hold back his shout of surprise. Despite his lack of energy he bucked his hips, desperate to tip over into the abyss.

"Don't tell me you don't love this." She stroked the hidden gland that turned his cock into living steel.

He was a kite twisting in the wind, flying higher and higher only to spiral down in a dizzying spin then jerking back up to soar higher.

His throat grew sore from his strangled groans. "I'm going to come."

Her husky reply shredded the last of his control. "Give yourself to me."

All of the energy in the world gathered in his chest before exploding in a ball of light and heat, robbing all of his senses except for the heat shooting out of his cock and the sensation of her wet mouth sucking him dry.

It wasn't until Brett tucked the cool sheet up to his neck that he realized he'd blacked out. Through half-opened eyes he saw that she had dressed and was pulling on her coat. His arms were still pinned over his head, the chain wrapped neat and tidy around his muscles like the stripes on a candy cane.

"What are you doing?"

"I'm securing our future."

When she turned to leave, panic brought him fully alert. "Brett, come back here. You are not going out there alone. Brett." He spat curses in several languages and pulled at the cuffs. "Do not think for a moment that this will stop me from coming after you. Brett!"

The click of her boots traveled farther down the hall, then nothing but silence as the door slammed and the lock clicked in place.

Chapter Twelve

DID SHE FEEL any guilt leaving Kristos naked and cuffed to her bed? Hell no.

Well, maybe a smidgen. But the man had to learn to let her fight her own battles.

When she arrived at the station the morning roll call was in progress, which allowed her to sneak undetected to her office. With a brush in hand, she went into the bathroom to tidy her appearance and gasped at her reflection. The brush fell to the floor, scattering across the tile.

"Holy shit," she breathed and leaned closer to the mirror to examine the pale jade-green of her eyes.

She completed the bond. What the hell did that mean now?

Kristos said mated pairs could sense the other's emotions no matter the distance between them. Would he be a living entity inside her, guiding, arguing and influencing her decisions? Was he in her mind now?

"Kristos?" she whispered, reaching out with all of her awareness.

Nothing, absolutely nothing, which frightened her more

than the thought of having him in her head. Perhaps the chain weakened their emotional connection as well.

She shook away the panic that flared with that thought. Yeah, she was definitely going to call Lucian to release him. An hour, she just needed an hour to begin securing her future not only as sheriff, but also with the man she loved.

After she dressed it took only a few moments at the computer to launch the tracking program given to her by her contact in the city. Once she baited the trap she knew Neimi would be contacted, exposing the rats in the department. She linked the program to her Smartphone and set out to collect the vermin.

Roll call was wrapping up as she strode into the break room with a swagger loaded with confidence. "Good morning, gentlemen. Deputy Joyce." She nodded to the one female in attendance.

Collins greeted her with a raised brow. "Morning, Sheriff. I didn't expect to see you so early. I heard you were here pretty late last night."

"You know what they say about crime never sleeping. May I take the floor?"

"Certainly." Collins stepped to the side.

"I've received the warrant to arrest Jebadiah Neimi on suspicion of illegal mining and collusion. Ottley and Jax will stay in town to respond to all other calls, everyone else will assist me with the arrest. Neimi may be one man, but he thinks he's king shit. Once he realizes he's losing his crown he may panic and become unpredictable. We strike after the shift change at the quarry. Here's where I want everyone to set up."

On the white board she drew a rudimentary diagram of the layout of the area and assigned her men their positions. A charge of excitement lifted the hair on her arms as the deputies realized she was serious and for the first time in years they were going on a real, honest-to-God, takedown.

"Team A heads out in fifteen. Team B rolls out in thirty. Do not draw attention that something is going down and stay alert. We convene at the location at six a.m. Good luck."

Once the room cleared she headed for her squad car, reaching for her cell as she climbed inside. The other line picked up on the first ring. "Alpha team, the ball's in play. Stand by for my signal."

"10-4, Sheriff."

The cell vibrated as she ended the call. She looked at the display and felt the bile of betrayal rise in her throat. The trap was sprung. The time had come to arrest some of her own.

✦　✦　✦

"BY THE GODS, brother, this is the saddest sight I have ever seen."

Kristos cracked open eyelids that felt as if they were caked in rubber cement. "Kill me now," he murmured with a grimace, or at least he thought he made the muscles in his face twitch. He was so weak that it taxed his reserves to move that little bit. Was it a blessing or a curse that Lucian was here to see him handcuffed to a bed and stretched out naked like a human sacrifice? A prime example of the stupidity of a man who let his cock out-think his brain.

Lucian took a moment to survey the sorry scene. "Oh how I wish I had a camera."

A growl rumbled from Kristos' throat, a vain attempt to show some sign of strength. To his further humiliation, it came out more like a feeble moan. "Just release me."

"That woman of yours is resourceful. I could have used her as a royal guard." Lucian chuckled at his brother's horrified gasp. "Brains, strength, beauty. She would have made a fine assassin."

Kristos swallowed a strangled groan, not wanting to encourage his brother. The only thing royal Brett was going to experience was an ass paddling. He still couldn't believe she would use her sexual power over him to drain his abilities. It was sneaky, underhanded and he wished he thought of it first. Then he'd be the one to put a stop to the threat against her.

Lucian unwrapped the chain from around Kristos' arms and raced with it out of the room. When he strolled back in at a much slower pace, a smarmy grin curled his lips and his eyes twinkled with the laughter Kristos was now able to sense he was dying to release. "How did you come to this predicament?"

Ignoring his brother's question, Kristos focused on bending his wrists to better grip the chain linking the cuffs. His fingers felt as substantial as marshmallows as he struggled to grip the metal. With a frustrated sigh he clanged the cuffs against the bedframe. "Uncuff me. Now."

"I think I'll let you break out once your strength returns." He crossed his arms. "Did you let her do this willingly?"

"I have no problem with maiming you if you don't release me now."

"Ah, come on Krissy. I have such few pleasures in my life. Let me have this one. No?" He raised a brow when Kristos continued to stare at him with all of the anger, humiliation and worry he funneled into an arrow straight at his heart. "Oh, all right."

Lucian grasped the chain between the cuffs and snapped it in two like a twig. Kristos groaned as the circulation returned to his arms like a million fire ants crawling over his skin.

"How are you feeling?"

"Like a *boarhund* shit me out then stepped on me." He swung his legs over the edge of the bed and rose slowly to stand. The world spun, buckling his knees and causing him to collapse back onto the mattress.

"You've felt worse." His brother pointed out.

"What is with you today?" He couldn't stop the cranky petulance that colored his tone.

"It is the joy of new experiences. For instance, I've never experienced this before." Lucian grinned joyfully as he held up his phone. "A text from your sheriff that says, 'Your brother is at my house and needs your assistance. Please be kind'. To say I was intrigued would be an understatement."

"She must have the evidence to go after Neimi and doesn't want me to interfere, otherwise she wouldn't have gone to such lengths to prevent me from doing just that. Silly girl. It's my honor to protect her."

"Brother, is it more important for you to be right or for her to be yours?"

What little energy he regained was instantly deflated at Lucian's words. In his hearts he knew that he would have to let Brett steer her own course, but the male in him fought that reality as vehemently as she fought his interference. "I'm afraid to lose her."

"Then let her fly. She'll come back to you." Lucian tilted his head from side to side. A considering frown crinkled his brow. "I'm not sure I can get used to you being a blond."

"What?" He stumbled to his feet and staggered to the mirror over the dresser. His hearts raced at the sight of the honey-blond hair that curled around his ears. The bond was complete. Brett was his mate.

"Congratulations." Lucian handed him his clothes.

"Thanks." He pulled on his jeans, still distracted by his new appearance, then he ran both hands through his hair and doubled over with a groan. "How can I not go after her now?"

"Can you sense her?"

He slowed his breathing and stood still. Borrowing from the well of Lucian's serenity and steadfastness, he reached out with his powers, sifting through the sea of emotions of the people in the town to hone in on the one whose signature matched his own.

"I found her." His eyes flew open and he rubbed at an ache that settled behind his sternum. "She's...sad."

"Is she hurt?"

"No, just sad. I have to help her." He finished tugging on the rest of his clothes.

"What do you have planned so that I can interject a thread of sanity?" Lucian held up a hand to stop the interruption that had sprung to his lips. "She's my sister now. I don't want anything to harm her either, but we must be rational."

Kristos absorbed the affection Lucian had for Brett and relaxed with the knowledge that between the two of them she would be safe. "If she has the evidence to arrest Neimi, she must also know, or least has a suspicion, about who on her team is working against her."

Lucian nodded and began to pace. "That may explain why she is sad. I know how difficult it is when someone you have trusted betrays you." Their eyes met in a brief moment of remembrance. "If you were Brett, what would you do?"

He smiled at the thought of what hell she'd bring down. "Go right up to Neimi and face him like a warrior."

"Who would you have as backup?"

"My most trusted men, and at least one traitor to lead the way and to make an example of."

"Of course." Lucian's smile widened. Kristos wondered if he knew that his posture straightened into the stance he used as the Head of the Guard. As stern a taskmaster as there ever was. "So what will you do?"

"Observe from a distance and interfere only when necessary."

Lucian clapped him on the back. "You can be taught." He held up a finger and crossed to the door. "I have something for you."

He gaped in shock as Lucian tossed him his royal uniform. "What about maintaining a low profile?"

"We are all learning how to do what is right and not necessarily about being right."

"Thank you, Lucian."

"Thanks nothing. I'll be right beside you."

His bark of laughter hurt his throat. "I knew it. The Chameleon is too powerful to resist."

"I wouldn't say that, but your woman is in need and I will provide help." He held out his hand with his fingers curled in a half circle.

Kristos slid his palm along his brother's then locked their fingers together to form a tight circle. They released their hold then gripped each other around the forearm and bent at the waist in a short bow.

The *Llanos* brothers were on the mission.

Chapter Thirteen

"JIMINY CHRISTMAS," BRETT muttered when she spotted her men on the forest floor a hundred yards outside Neimi's personal residence.

Six of her most-trusted deputies lay flat on their bellies with their elbows bent to hold binoculars or night vision goggles to their eyes. With black and green makeup smudged over their faces, they looked like life-sized plastic army men.

Reutgers spotted her first, flashing a series of hand gestures that made absolutely no sense. She knelt next to him and tightened the straps on the Kevlar vest around her chest. "When was the last time you all trained on stakeouts and takedowns?"

"Billings didn't think we had enough crime to warrant the expense."

She rolled her eyes. "Of course. Update please."

"Lights came on about twenty minutes ago. No one's gone in or out but there's been a lot of shouting," he reported.

"Who's inside?"

"Neimi and a woman."

"His wife?"

"Nope, she left at about twenty-two hundred hours with a suitcase. This one arrived about thirty minutes later."

"Sister, niece?"

His cheeks turned pink enough to be seen in the twilight.

"I don't think so."

Ewww, she gagged.

The intel she gathered revealed that Billings and four others had received the same amount of pat at the same time from accounts traced to the Neimi family. Three of her deputies were easy to identify for they all banked with the tiny family-operated Cedar Savings and Loan. It was either arrogance or lack of knowledge about current technology that made them forget that with a few keystrokes, one's entire livelihood became an open book to whoever had the knowhow.

But the fourth person, Colleen Bastian, was still a mystery. She never served on the force nor was she a spouse of an officer. She also didn't hold an account at the bank. There wasn't a connection to anyone in Cedar other than the fact she received the same payout from Neimi that was distributed by the bank manager.

Brett staged the fake operation at the quarry hoping one of the potential suspects would warn their benefactor and reveal themselves in the process. Fifteen minutes had passed since the alert went to her phone that Neimi had been contacted by someone on her squad. It was a call she anticipated, but it didn't soften the blow that one of her own betrayed her.

The group went still as the front door opened and a young

woman ran out dressed only in a bright-white bra and mini-skirt. She picked up a rock and threw it at the front window. "Screw you, Jeb. That's for the hundred you still owe me."

"Just get out," he bellowed from inside.

Brett snickered. This was turning out to be a hell of a morning.

As the unknown trick took off down the lane in a plume of exhaust and gravel, Brett's phone buzzed softly with an incoming call. A smug grin stole across her lips as she answered, "Mr. Neimi, you're up awfully early."

"Sheriff Briggs, it seems that there's been a little misunderstanding." A touch of panic edged the smooth delivery.

"About what?"

"I heard there's a warrant out for my arrest, which is completely uncalled for. I suggest you and I meet to discuss these allegations before you embark on an endeavor that could ruin your career."

"Well, Mr. Neimi, I've gathered lots of evidence that I'll be happy to show your lawyer. You can discuss strategy with Judge Mancini, who you will be sharing a holding cell with until you're transferred to County. I'd normally suggest you call Terrance Neely at the bank to arrange your bail but he'll be sitting beside you as well."

"You're making a mistake, sweetheart. One that will cost you more than your job."

"Bring it on." She disconnected the call and swirled her finger in the air, signaling the troops to move. "He's running scared. We go in now. Ready?" At their nod, she took the lead down the hill.

Four deputies circled 'round the front of the house while she approached the back door with Reutgers and Tyson, who carried a battering ram. She raised her hand and counted down. Three...two...one.

The oak door gave way in a shower of splinters with one solid stroke. Brett barreled through the kitchen with her weapon drawn. From the front of the house she heard the crash of wood and glass as the others stormed the entry. In the noise and confusion her training kicked in, helping her maintain a laser-like focus on the movement of every man as they searched the first floor.

They found Neimi in his study next to an open wall safe. A duffle bag lay at his feet, overflowing with bundles of cash.

"Hands in the air," she shouted. "Hands in the air now!"

He dropped the strap in his hands and slowly raised his hands. "Sheriff, what a surprise."

"You're under arrest." She holstered her weapon and spun Neimi around, slamming him face first onto the desk. She cuffed his wrists behind his back and read him his rights.

"It doesn't have to be this way." He talked over her. "I can offer you a deal better than Billings. And your men too. I can pay you all. In cash. Over there." He gestured with his head. "Five hundred thousand dollars. Take it. And there's more. I can be reasonable."

Brett didn't like the way her men eyed the stack of cash on

the floor. That was a lot of money for a little bit of effort. She'd have to move fast to make sure their consciences won out over their pockets.

"I take it you're forgoing your right to remain silent?" She grabbed him by the back of the collar and shoved him toward the door.

His arrogant smirk remained despite the rough treatment. "My word is good. Isn't it, Deputy Collins?"

Brett turned to see Collins standing outside the broken front door. "Colleen Bastian, I presume?"

He flushed red. "How did you know?"

She pointed to her phone. "There's an app for everything."

It was a joke made when the last thing she felt like doing was laughing. A piece of her died on the inside as she forced the words out of her tight throat. "Mick Collins, you're under arrest."

He chuckled and scratched his chin. His eyes glinted with a hint of hysteria as he nodded. "Not today."

In a blink he darted out the door. She gave chase and stopped short at the sight of three pickup trucks pulling into the yard. Men armed with giant wrenches, chains and rifles spilled out of the cabs.

"Inside the house," she directed and pushed the remains of the door shut. "Stay away from the windows and keep him in the corner."

She shoved Neimi toward Reutgers and took a careful peek through the gap in the wood.

"Obviously the situation is spiraling out of your control, Sheriff," Neimi taunted. "We can end this right now if you let me go."

"The only way this is going to end is with all of you under arrest. Or dead," she murmured the last part under her breath.

The rag-tag group of men standing in sloppy formation in front of the house weren't soldiers. They were laborers, working men. Greed or fear of losing their jobs brought them here. She'd bet her last tan blouse that the most action these men ever saw was the occasional bar brawl when a Steelers' fan dared root against the Seahawks. They were untried and inexperienced. Complete wildcards that made for a potential deadly standoff.

Dear Lord, give me strength and a sign this won't end in horrible carnage.

An electrical charge zipped across the back of her neck and the hair on her arms stood on end.

She bit back a curse even as she thanked the heavens. "Be on the ready, boys. A storm is about to roll in and he's really pissed."

Chapter Fourteen

B RETT FORCED HER lungs to take slow, deep breaths as a tempest of anticipation built.

Outside, Neimi's men began to twitch as if they were being jolted with a cattle prod. They twirled in circles, searching the dark depths of the woods for signs of the imminent attack. Inside, her deputies braced themselves against the walls, unaware that the rumble they felt was coming from one seriously angry alien.

She reached out with her mind, testing their connection in the best way she knew how. The source of Kristos' energy was a weak flicker but a connection nonetheless. She concentrated on warning him of the danger and to reassure him that she was safe.

His fear for her left a bitter taste on her tongue but there was also a sweet hint of faith. He believed in her. He was there to help, not take over. If it meant saving lives, she'd gladly accept whatever assistance he offered.

She turned toward her troops. "Reutgers, stay with Neimi. If you lose him, it's your job. Everyone else, when you see men start to fall I want them cuffed before they think about calling for backup."

"What's going down, Sheriff?" Tyson asked.

"We're about to get a little help."

"From who?"

"The Chameleon."

At the sound of his name, a flurry of leaves kicked up in a straight line heading directly for the group of miners.

Bursts of light sparkled around the Chameleon where the reflection from the headlights hit the multicolored tunic covering his torso. His blurred image left tracers that reminded Brett of a movie where someone took a hit of acid and the world slowed even as it went a million miles an hour.

At ten against one, the miners were still no match against the Chameleon. A few got in a lucky punch but soon they began to drop like bags of sand, clutching broken arms or shattered jaws.

"Let's go. Let's go," Brett barked. "Watch your backs."

From the corner of her eye she spotted Collins racing for the thick shelter of trees and followed right on his ass.

The heavy canopy above blocked the morning light, forcing her to watch her step through the tangle of vines and ferns. Using an evergreen for cover, she palmed her Glock with both hands as she strained to hear over her pounding heart.

Silence. A deep silence that made her skin pebble under a layer of sweat.

He was hiding. Was he hoping to wait her out until he was clear to escape or preparing to launch an ambush?

To her right a branch cracked like a bullwhip through the silence. A gunshot followed that came from far to the left.

She clenched her teeth to hold back a curse. *Kristos. Goddammit.*

"Hey, Collins," she shouted and rolled to the next tree, hoping to split his attention. "So who's Colleen Bastian? Ex-girlfriend? Favorite hooker?"

"Shut up." Another gunshot. The bullet ricocheted off the tree to her side. "She was my foster mother."

"Is she proud that you're a disgrace to the badge?" She bent to pick up a rock and tossed it deeper into the woods.

"Shut up!"

A loud crash and a muffled shout erupted. Brett risked a glance around her cover.

Kristos and Collins were a tangle of limbs as they rolled on the ground, fighting for possession of the gun. Plants and roots twisted around their legs as they muscled each other for dominance. Kristos' rolling rage hit her like a blast furnace in the cold. Only the solid bands of justice tempered his powers, reining in the urge to permanently incapacitate the suspect.

Brett crept closer with her weapon trained on the writhing bodies, waiting for an opening to assist.

Her blood froze as she watched Collins rise up in triumph with the gun in hand. He took aim and fired.

Kristos yelped, reaching for his shoulder as he fell to the forest floor.

Brett reacted without hesitation as years of training kicked in. She fired off two rounds in quick succession. She was taught to aim for the chest and she didn't miss. Collins collapsed before the sound of her shot stopped echoing through the forest.

Keeping her weapon on Collins, she raced to Kristos' side. His eyes were shut tight with the pain she felt burning down her arm through their bond. His skin grew pale, glowing whitest around his pinched mouth. "Kristos, sweetie, talk to me."

"I'm fine," he gritted. "I think the bullet went clean through." He opened his eyes, capturing hers with his sad gaze. "Go to him. He needs you."

She looked over to Collins who lay limp in the ferns. "Stay put. Don't be a hero."

"I won't."

Once she was satisfied that all weapons were out of reach, she holstered her gun and knelt in the dirt. To her horror the front of his coat was soaked and a trickle of blood leaked from his mouth.

"Son of a bitch," she shouted and pulled at his clothes until she got to bare skin covered in blood. "Where's your vest? Dammit, Mick. Where's your vest!"

"Did. You. Had. To," he panted. "Made you."

She stripped off her coat and pressed it to his wounds in a vain attempt to stop the inevitable. "You fucking son of a bitch. Was it worth it? Huh, was it?"

A bit of blood sprayed as he laughed. "No."

What a waste. What a fucking waste. The moment he drew his pistol he knew what she would do and he did it anyway. And for what, money? He threw his life away for five hundred an acre. Why didn't he come to her? She would have helped him. If he weren't dying, she would've beaten him silly for making such a stupid choice.

"I so hate you right now." She reached for her radio and struggled to hold on to the plastic in her slippery grip. "This is Sheriff Briggs. I need a medic in the woods to the west of the Neimi residence stat. Officer down. Repeat. Officer down to the west of the Neimi residence." Her voice conveyed complete command as big, fat tears rolled down her cheeks and dripped to mingle with the blood on her hands.

"Brett. No." Collins tried to reach for her but dropped his hand. "No tears for me."

"You need help."

"I'm sorry," he whispered. "I'm so sorry."

"Me too, oh God, me too."

"Don't be." He managed a weak smile.

Under her hold, his legs jerked and a long breath rattled out of his lungs. The light slowly faded from his blue eyes until he stared vacantly up at the gray sky.

Great painful sobs ripped from her soul. She clenched her teeth tight to hold them at bay but they continued to rip in guttural bursts that tore at her throat. The only other time she took a life was during a high-speed chase of a drug runner that ended with the suspect opening fire on the road block she was part of. She'd been called a hero then. Even received a medal.

But this wasn't another criminal. Collins had been a trusted partner, a brother. Now he was dead because he was stupid and that pissed her off.

"Brett, it's not your fault."

A warm sensation settled over her back, leaching the coldness that pooled in her gut and replacing it with love and understanding.

"Shit, Kristos." She crawled to his side. "I'm sorry. Sweetie, how are you doing?"

"It's not your fault, *alskata*." He reached for her hand. "He was well aware of the consequences of his actions."

"I know. But it still sucks. It sucks…hard." She kissed the center of his palm. "We need to get you to a doctor."

"I'll take care of him." Lucian came into view dressed like the Chameleon. "Paramedics will be here soon. We need to go."

She squeezed Kristos' hand tighter. "He needs a hospital. He's been shot."

"Don't worry, sister. I've field dressed my share of battle wounds." He scooped an arm under Kristos and helped him to his feet. "Your man will be waiting for you to return. On my honor."

Kristos brushed the backs of his fingers down her cheek. "Will you be all right?"

"Eventually." She pressed a kiss to his lips and whispered, "I love you."

His smile went a long way in healing her heart. "I know."

"Aren't you a smart one? If that wound starts to fester, you get to a hospital immediately."

"Yes ma'am."

After a last kiss on Kritsos' lips, the brothers left her alone. She walked back to Collins and said a silent goodbye to the man who was once her friend.

✦　✦　✦

KRISTOS SMILED UP at her from his seat on the couch and opened his arms. "Welcome home, *alskata*. Come rest by me."

Brett collapsed by his side and brushed away his hug to examine the puckered mark on his bare chest. "The truth. How are you?"

"I'll heal." He pulled her into his embrace. "I heard you've put the fear of God into the good people of Cedar. Your authority has been firmly established."

"Yeah that's me, the big, badass sheriff." She burrowed deeper into his heat and closed her eyes. She earned the town's respect but the cost was difficult to bear.

"You are the bravest woman in the universe. I'm so proud of you."

"Don't, please. What I did wasn't brave and it certainly isn't something to be proud of."

He drew back and tilted her chin up. The fire in his eyes matched the pulse of heat radiating from her core and up between her breasts, wrapping her in its magic. "It's not what you did but how you did it. You acted with courage and honor, like a true leader. You are a warrior, Brett, and I'm proud that you are my warrior."

His kiss brought tears to her eyes. Here she was safe. Here in his arms she was able to let go and feel, cry and be the woman she wasn't allowed to be in public. Kristos' love gave her that precious gift and she was almost stupid enough to turn him away.

"Thank you for loving me."

"It's my honor, *alskata*."

She brushed her fingers through his thick golden hair and cupped his nape, smiling. "Blond, huh?"

He grabbed her hand and pressed a kiss in the center. "Yep."

"How long will this bond last?"

"Forever, if that's all right with you."

She nestled deeper into his arms. "Will that be long enough?"

"Perhaps. I owe you for sending my brother to find me in a humiliating situation. I'm going to need a lot of time once I get you in these."

He held up his hand and dangled a shiny new pair of handcuffs.

She bit her lip to suppress a giggle. Pressing her tender breasts again his chest, she brushed a kiss along his jaw. "Admit it. You liked being at my mercy."

"You are a menace to my manhood. It's going to take me

all night, and most of tomorrow, to properly punish you for the slight."

This time she let her laughter burst forth and reached down to squeeze the hard length straining the zipper of his jeans. "Impressive weapon you've got there. But you've forgotten something."

"What's that?" he stuttered on a breathy gasp.

She scraped her nails down his erection, which made him hiss and buck against her hand. She plucked the cuffs from his weak grip and jumped to her feet, swinging her prize with a triumphant laugh. "I'm not without my own powers."

He stalked after her, slow and lethal, stripping off his jeans and revealing how ready he was to make good on his threat. "You're going down, Briggs."

"Make me," she taunted with a swipe of her tongue along her lower lip that ended with a startled scream as he closed the distance in a blink of an eye and tossed her over his shoulder.

She ran an appreciative hand over his naked ass and relaxed in his hold. She'd allow this caveman behavior, this time. If need be, there was always a chain of molybdenite tucked under the mattress. Just in case.

About Anna Alexander

Anna Alexander is the award winning author of the Heroes of Saturn and the Sprawling A Ranch series. With Hugh Jackman's abs and Christopher Reeve's blue eyes as inspiration, she loves spinning tales of superheroes finding love. Anna also loves to give back and has served on the board for the Greater Seattle Romance Writers of America as chapter president and on the committee for the Emerald City Writers Conference.

Sign up to receive news about Anna's latest releases at:

http://eepurl.com/Q0tsz

Website

annaalexander.net

Facebook

facebook.com/pages/Anna-Alexander/282170065189471

Twitter

twitter.com/AnnaWriter

Newsletter

http://eepurl.com/Q0tsz

Also by Anna Alexander

Heroes of Saturn Series

Hero Revealed

Hero Unleashed

Hero Unmasked

Hero Rising

Men of the Sprawling A Ranch Series

The Cowboy Way

The Marlboro Man

To Have Faith

Elite Metal

Bound by Steele

Adamantium's Roar

Elite Ghosts

Thallium's Submission

Made in the USA
Charleston, SC
26 February 2016